W9-AMT-581

White River Regional Library
368 E. Main Str
Batesville, AR 72501

DISCARD

Independence County Library
368 E. Main Street
Batesville, AR 72501

'And who,' Drake asked softly, 'is Simon?'

Olivia tamped down incipient hysteria. 'Simon is your son.'

Astonishment glittered in the cold eyes before being banished so completely that Olivia wondered whether she had seen aright. Oh, he was a brilliant actor! If she didn't know better, she thought bitterly, she'd believe he hadn't known of the child he'd fathered the year she was seventeen.

Olivia Nicholls and the two half-sisters Anet and Jan Carruthers are all born survivors—but, so far, unlucky in love. Things change, however, when an eighteenth-century miniature portrait of a beautiful and mysterious young woman passes into each of their hands. It may be coincidence, it may not! The portrait is meant to be a charm to bring love to the lives of those who possess it—but there is one condition:

I found Love as you'll find yours,
and trust it will be true,
This Portrait is a fated charm
To speed your Love to you.

But if you be not Fortune's Fool
Once your Heart's Desire is nigh,
Pass on my likeness as Cupid's Tool
Or your Love will fade and die.

Recent titles by Robyn Donald:

TIGER EYES
ELEMENT OF RISK
PRINCE OF LIES

THE
MIRROR BRIDE

BY
ROBYN DONALD

White River Regional Library
368 E. Main Street
Batesville, AR 72501

Independence County Library
368 E. Main Street
Batesville, AR 72501

DISCARD

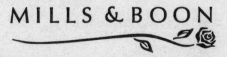

MILLS & BOON

For Frances Whitehead. Thank you.

All the characters in this book have no existence outside the imagination of the author, and have no relation whatsoever to anyone bearing the same name or names. They are not even distantly inspired by any individual known or unknown to the author, and all the incidents are pure invention.

All rights reserved including the right of reproduction in whole or in part in any form. This edition is published by arrangement with Harlequin Enterprises II B.V. The text of this publication or any part thereof may not be reproduced or transmitted in any form or by any means, electronic or mechanical, including photocopying, recording, storage in an information retrieval system, or otherwise, without the written permission of the publisher.

MILLS & BOON and the Rose Device
are trademarks of the publisher.
Harlequin Mills & Boon Limited,
Eton House, 18-24 Paradise Road, Richmond, Surrey TW9 1SR

© Robyn Donald 1996

ISBN 0 263 14807 6

Set in Times Roman 10 on 11 pt.
07-9608-57840 C1

Made and printed in Great Britain

97 3624

CHAPTER ONE

SHE was very young.

Olivia didn't know her, but the beautiful face was familiar. Something, she thought hazily, about the surprisingly square jaw and the determined mouth—a mouth now set in a straight line.

'Write to him,' the unknown woman directed, the ribbons and feathers in her headdress swaying as she gave a swift, decisive nod of her elaborately styled head. Bright blue eyes commanded Olivia's attention. 'It is the only thing you can do now. You *must* write.'

'I can't!'

The sound of her own voice woke her. Blearily she lifted her head to gaze with slowly clearing vision around the small, shabby room. Of course no lovely young woman stood there, dressed in the frills and lace and silk of the middle of the eighteenth century. This room was definitely twentieth-century, from the faded, bargain-basement vinyl on the floor to the garishly painted wooden cupboards above and below the sink bench.

While sitting at the battered Formica table and poring over calculations that had kept her awake for nights, Olivia had gone to sleep and dreamed—a remarkably vivid dream, but in reality just a dramatisation of the decision she had already made, a decision she didn't want to face.

So her subconscious had made her acknowledge it.

Yawning, she pushed a lock of honey-blonde hair back from her face. Her capable, long-fingered hand came down abruptly on the sheet of paper she had covered with figures, then curled, strangely vulnerable. Head bowed, she joined her hands loosely, looking at nothing in particular with great, lacklustre topaz eyes. Almost immediately she firmed her soft mouth, pulled a cheap, thin writing pad towards her and began to write, only to stop after two sentences.

'Oh, that won't do; it's too stupid,' she muttered, glowering at the stamp she'd already stuck onto the envelope—a tiny rock wren delicately depicted in shades of buff and black and gold.

Her eyes lingered on the words along the bottom: 'New Zealand', it said. '45c'.

Forty-five cents she couldn't really afford.

Seed money, she thought, grimacing before she returned to writing the most difficult letter of her life.

Several times she stopped to frown more deeply, chewing on the end of the ballpoint pen and staring blindly through the window. On the other side of the busy street a row of run-down shops was topped by flats like the one she lived in, their windows reflecting blankly back at her.

There was no inspiration to be gained there. Or anywhere. After almost an hour spent crossing out and rewriting, she at last decided on the bare minimum.

Dear Drake,
I need to see you. There is something you should know.

And she signed it his faithfully, Olivia Nicholls.

It sounded faintly sinister, but that couldn't be helped. Explicitness was impossible because there was always the chance of someone else—a wife, for example—seeing the letter.

Quickly, because although she'd spent days agonising over this she still wasn't sure she was doing the right thing, Olivia sealed the envelope, then ran with it down the rickety outside stairs to the grimy street below. She'd give him a fortnight—no more and no less. If he hadn't answered by then, she'd have to step up her campaign.

Auckland at the fag-end of autumn was depressing. Autumn meant that winter was not far behind, and winter meant earache and the dreaded Auckland cough, which in Simon invariably turned to bronchitis. Winter meant nightmares about trying to dry and air clothes. It meant expensive vegetables and the pain of seeing Simon go off to school in inadequate clothing.

For the last three years she and Simon had lived in Auckland, and this third winter was promising to be worse than the two previous ones. Only five days ago she'd lost her job as an outworker sewing tracksuits for a factory. It hadn't brought in much, but the small amount had supplemented the unemployment benefit which was now all they had to live on. Saving money would be impossible. And there was the crushing debt she owed Brett, her next-door neighbour...

And, to cap off the series of disasters, she'd developed a rotten head cold.

She stopped outside the letterbox, looking down at the address on the envelope. You don't have to send it, a voice reminded her—a cautious, cowardly voice. You can struggle on—nobody dies of starvation in New Zealand.

Her eyes lingered on her hands. Once they had been pampered and smooth, the fingernails polished; now the fingernails were cut straight across and the skin was slightly chapped, marred by calluses from the constant use of scissors. Had she seen them, her mother would have had a fit. Elizabeth Harley had considered it part of her purpose in life to be elegant and well-groomed. She would have thought that Olivia was letting down the side.

But then, Elizabeth had been the indulged only daughter of a rich man, whereas Olivia had no money at all.

A shiver ran down her spine. What she was doing was dangerous, but there was no alternative. Defiantly she pushed the letter into the slot.

Trying to banish the matter to the back of her mind— it was done, she had made the decision and now she'd just have to wait—she set off to pick Simon up from school.

As she came down the street he burst through the gateway like a prisoner released from long incarceration, a too-thin six-year-old in the throes of a growing spurt. Olivia's eyes lingered on his bony wrists. He'd already outgrown the clothes she'd made for him at the beginning of summer, and although she had shopped carefully the year before at the winter sales, making sure that the two jerseys and the jacket were a size larger than she'd thought necessary, she suspected he was almost too big for them too.

If that letter worked, she thought wearily, she'd no longer need to worry about money to buy the shoes they both needed. If it didn't work—well, she'd go without, and his would be bought from the op-shop.

The letter had to work.

Banishing the odd little clutch of fear in her stomach, she smiled down at Simon.

'Hello, Liv,' he said, incandescently delighted at being freed from school.

'Hello, young Simon,' she said, speaking clearly. 'Have you had a good day?'

A year ago he used to hold her hand down the street, but she knew better than to hold it out now.

'Mrs Adams sent a note home.' Although belligerence darkened eyes the same colour and shape as hers, she caught a glimmer of wistfulness before he looked away.

'Oh, Simon!'

'I haven't been naughty,' he shouted, kicking a stone. 'It's about a trip to the beach. I said I couldn't go but she said I had to take it home anyway.'

Both of them hated those notes—Olivia because it was so rarely that she could afford the promised trip, and Simon because his absence made him an outcast amongst his peers. Even in this poor area most families were better off then they were.

Until she'd begun saving for his ear operation she had always managed to find the money to send him away with the rest of his class. She had explained why he could no longer go, but when you weren't much over six, and all your friends teased you about staying behind, it was difficult to comprehend the need to save money. Especially as he didn't really understand that he was going deaf.

'Hand it over,' she said.

He did, but before she had a chance to read it asked, 'Liv, why do we speak different?'

'Differently,' she said automatically. 'From whom?'

'Well, everyone. I had a fight with Sean Singleton today 'cause he said I was up myself, talking like the Poms. Are we Poms?'

'No, we're not English. You speak the way you do because that's how I talk.' She didn't really know what to say. Although New Zealand believed itself to be a classless society, it was untrue. End up with no money and you were automatically relegated to the bottom of the heap. And if you lived on a benefit with a child and no husband you became a solo mother, the subject of smug, middle-class disdain.

Not looking at her, he mumbled, 'Sean said I was a dummy.'

'You know that's not true. As soon as we get your ears fixed you'll show Sean Singleton that you're every bit as clever as he is. Until then, darling, try not to fight.' A glance at his mutinous expression made her ask with a sinking heart, 'What else happened?'

Children could be so cruel—little animals picking mercilessly on anyone who was the slightest bit different. A sunny-tempered child, Simon had adored school when he first started, but it was an effort to get him there now. His teacher did what she could, but she had a big class and the school was under-resourced.

'Nothing,' he muttered. 'I don't care about Sean Singleton. I can beat him any time. Aren't you going to read the note?'

The school was planning an overnight trip to the marine reserve at Leigh, sixty miles up the coast. Unless Drake accepted the responsibility he'd avoided these last seven years there was no way she could take money out of her bank account for a school trip. Not now, when she had no job and little hope of getting one.

Unfortunately she couldn't tell Simon that; if Drake refused to acknowledge his obligations Simon would be all the more shattered for having had the prospect held out to him.

Olivia slipped the note into her pocket.

Simon's eyes followed her hand. Angrily he said, 'I knew it would cost too much.' He hid his disappointment too well for a child of six. 'We better go home and fold some papers.'

They spent some hours each week folding a variety of advertising pamphlets which he and Olivia delivered around the district. The money it earned used to pay for the meagre luxuries they couldn't have afforded otherwise, but from now on it would all go towards necessities.

Olivia's whole being rose up in hot resentment. It simply wasn't fair that Simon should be denied most of the things his classmates took for granted, that he should live in a grotty first-floor flat with no garden except an unmown stretch of grass cluttered by a clothesline, three car bodies and a lemon tree that struggled to survive from year to year. It wasn't fair that he had to wear clothes she made from cheap remnants or hunted for in opportunity shops and end-of-season sales. It wasn't fair that his life should be so circumscribed, that he should be unable to take advantage of the many things New Zealand's biggest city offered.

But then, she'd learned that nothing in this life was fair. However, she thought, firming her mouth, she had taken the first steps to redress the balance for Simon.

Back home, she sent him to put his bag away while she drew a cup of hot water from the tap and squeezed a lemon into it. Sitting down to drink it, she watched him make a sandwich, and winced at the amount of peanut butter he spread on it. She bit back the unguarded protest. Simon wasn't greedy.

She wanted to take him places, to buy him books and toys to keep his active mind stretched—she yearned to give him some sort of future. Instead, he took their poverty for granted. It wouldn't have been so bad if she'd been able to claim the child benefits the country provided, but she didn't dare.

For Simon she would do anything, even sink her pride, because he was all she had.

Olivia pulled a sheet of newspaper across the table. It was about six weeks old, and she'd been lucky to get it. Brett always handed on his newspapers to her, but he very rarely bought them, preferring to get the news from the radio.

Her eyes were drawn to a photograph. Although she had spent too much of the last three days looking at it, her vision wavered, a sudden rush of blood to her head making her close her eyes.

Drake Arundell. A man she had known all her life, yet this man was a stranger.

Blinking swiftly, she forced her eyes open. Her gaze lingered on the hard face, its blunt contours set in an expression of assured authority. The seven years since she had seen him had added an air of maturity to his strong features. Power radiated from him, a power different from the untrammelled sexuality that had cut such a swathe through Springs Flat while he was growing up. Whatever had happened in those seven years had modified and strengthened the young man's arrogance into a disciplined self-reliance.

The boldly cut mouth was now controlled into a straight, uncompromising line, while level, enigmatic eyes surveyed the world from beneath black brows that winged up at the outer corners to give a saturnine expression to his face.

Those eyes were grey-green; when he was angry the green predominated, so that they became piercing slivers of crystal. Heavy-lidded, with thick, curly black lashes that didn't mitigate their inherent aloofness, they were astonishing eyes.

A formidable man, Drake Arundell, infinitely tougher and much more dangerous than the reckless, charismatic young man so vividly delineated in her memory. Just over six feet tall, he was in perfect proportion to his height, with a well-made smoothness of movement that satisfied the eye. He'd be—she made some quick calculations—about thirty-two, eight years older than she was.

Of course he'd be married by now. Men with his particular brand of virile masculine magnetism didn't stay single. And when they flashed across the motor racing scene like a singularly blatant comet, attracting the attention of film stars and models and any number of beautiful women, marriage usually followed. There were probably children too.

At seventeen, Olivia had responded to his heady, aggressive confidence as helplessly as most other women. More fool her, she thought sardonically.

'Have you got a headache?' Simon enquired around his peanut butter sandwich. 'You look funny.'

'Darling, swallow everything in your mouth before you talk. No, I'm fine.'

He came over to stand beside her. 'Who's that?'

'A man I used to know.' Had known all her life. 'He owns hotels and boats and things.' Her voice sounded quite normal.

Drake Arundell, the news item said, had announced the opening of the Tero ski-field. Three years ago Arundell had returned to New Zealand to buy the almost moribund FunNZ empire, and with a combination of shrewd, resourceful financial ability and an intuitive understanding of the tourism business had not only brought it back to life but expanded, without setting the powerful conservation movement at his throat.

The item went on to mention his spectacular reign as a Formula One driver, when he had been prevented from winning the Drivers' Championship only by injury. Drake Arundell had dropped out for five years before emerging to carve out an equally fast-moving career in the business world, being one of the first far-sighted enough to see the opportunity for the now world-famous eco-tours.

An unsteady wind blustered against the windows, streaking them with rain. A truck took its time about going by, changing gear with a jarring thump that rattled through Olivia's head. Shivering, she rubbed her arms to stir the circulation.

Her eyes returned to the photograph. The last time she'd seen him Drake Arundell had been furious, his striking face cold and unyielding, his eyes narrowed and savage beneath their half-closed lids.

It had happened so abruptly; they'd spent the summer playing a game of flirtation and retreat, and she'd loved it—enjoying the power of her burgeoning femininity enormously, discovering that life could be a fascinating, exhilarating feast of the senses.

Not once had he touched her, but she'd known that he watched her, that there was a different gleam in his eyes when he looked at her, an exciting intensity that wasn't there when he spoke to the other girls who had spent the summer trying to attract his attention.

And then one night after a barbecue at her parents' place he'd kissed her. Lost in the wonder of his kiss, she'd pressed against him. In three days' time he was going back to the Formula One circuits of the world, so this would be her only chance to see what it was like in his arms.

The gentle kiss had suddenly turned feral; she had gasped at the quick violence of his mouth, the way he'd held her against his hard, taut body, but she hadn't struggled. Although it frightened her she'd wanted that fierce, heated tension—had wanted it all summer.

But the kiss had ended abruptly. Strong hands pushed her away by the shoulders, leaving her aching with frustration.

'Don't offer more than you want to give,' he'd said in a thick, harsh voice. 'You've had your fun teasing me, but that's because I've let you. Don't make the mistake of thinking that another man would be so easily kept at bay.'

And he had looked at her as though he'd despised her.

It had happened a long time ago, but a long-forgotten fear sent a chill slithering the length of her backbone. Drake Arundell was not a man to be threatened or intimidated.

Unconsciously she angled her chin at the photograph. Why should he have his photograph in the newspapers as an example to other New Zealanders when she and Simon struggled for every cent they had?

Swallowing the last remnant of his sandwich, Simon washed his knife and plate and dried them carefully. 'I've got a new book,' he prompted as he put the dishes away.

Olivia screwed up the sheet of newspaper and fired it into the rubbish bin. 'We'd better fold these papers first,' she said. 'Then you can read to me.' Reading time was the one part of the evening that was sacrosanct.

He glanced out of the window and pulled a face. 'We'll get wet.'

The rain had settled in now, and was beating with miserable determination against the panes.

'It's all right,' she said. 'I don't have to do any more sewing, remember, so I can deliver them tomorrow morning.'

A fortnight later she'd almost accepted that Drake was going to ignore her letter, but after tidying the flat and exorcising some of her anger and frustration by viciously scrubbing the floor, she groaned when she looked at the battered alarm clock on the windowsill above the sink. Still another hour until the mail arrived.

'I'll go to the supermarket now, before it rains. And if a letter isn't waiting for me when I get back,' she said, baring her teeth at her reflection in the crazed mirror in the bathroom, 'somehow I'll come up with a way of making Drake Arundell's life an absolute hell!'

An hour later she arrived back home feeling completely wretched. Instead of hanging off until the afternoon as it was supposed to do, the rain had dumped icy gallons on her. By the time she made it back to the flat she was coughing, and although she'd fought her head cold with most of the lemons from the spindly tree in the communal back yard she had a horrible suspicion that the infection was sinking to her chest.

Money for cough syrup would be at the expense of food, but, she decided as she hung her drenched umbrella and skirt above the bath, she would deal with that worry when it arrived—if it did. After rubbing her hair reasonably dry with a threadbare towel, she changed into a pair of old pink sweatsuit trousers and sat down with a mug of hot lemon juice and water, listening to her breath rattle in her chest.

If something happened to her, Simon would be completely alone.

'The mail!' she said, suddenly leaping to her feet. A hectic dash down to the letterbox through the rain revealed two circulars and the power bill.

'Right,' she said through gritted teeth as she pounded back up the unprotected steps, the first cold southerly of the year tearing at her clothes and hair. 'Tonight I'm going to write you another letter, Drake Arundell, and it's going to be a lot harder to ignore. And if that doesn't work, I'll—I'll camp in your office until you agree to see me.'

Sudden, shameful tears clogged her throat; she swallowed and stubbornly set her mind to working out ways to apply pressure to a man who was determined to ignore her.

On her way to collect Simon from school she went into the corner dairy and again looked up under the As in the telephone directory. There was only one Arundell there—a D. Unless he was unlisted, it had to be Drake. When she had first seen his address she had been filled with a bitter, unpleasant resentment, because Judge's Bay was a very up-market suburb on the other side of Auckland.

Surreptitiously she compared the address with the copy she had made before. No, she hadn't made a mistake. Her mouth compressed into a straight line as she flipped through the pages to the Fs.

Drake Arundell wasn't going to get away with it. This time she'd write to him at both his address and the FunNZ one.

On her way out she stopped at the rack of brightly coloured magazines by the counter. TV STAR'S LOVE CHILD REVEALED, the headlines on one screamed. 'I AM DEVASTATED BY HIS INFIDELITY,' WEEPS MODEL bellowed another, beneath a picture of a woman who looked as though she wouldn't be able to pronounce any word of more than two syllables.

'Do you want one, miss?' the sari-clad owner said, stopping in her task of ripping the covers off several magazines.

Olivia smiled and shook her head, her eyes lingering on the gaudy covers. 'Are they very popular?'

'Oh, yes. These two—' she indicated the biggest headlines '—are running neck and neck.'

'You'd wonder at people who'd discuss their most intimate concerns with a journalist.'

The owner shrugged. 'I believe they pay well.'

And if you were desperate—as desperate, say, as she was, Olivia thought—then that money might be a good reason for baring your soul to the public of New Zealand.

Impulsively she asked, 'Could I have a cover?'

The woman looked surprised. 'Well, I tear them off any that haven't sold and send them back to the publisher so I don't have to pay for them.'

'Oh. I see.' Olivia looked at the magazines again. 'I didn't realise.' She smiled at the woman, said, 'Goodbye,' and left the shop.

The next morning she swept out the flat before embarking on the chore of washing their clothes; with any luck they'd dry enough to air in the hot water cupboard. A month previously the ancient agitator washing machine that lurked in the bathroom had clattered itself to a standstill, and although the landlord's agent had promised to replace it, a new one hadn't eventuated yet.

Determined to look on the bright side, Olivia admired the muscles she was developing in her arms as she hung the clothes out beneath a sky that promised at least a morning's fine weather. After that she boiled up the bones the butcher always gave her on the pretext that they were for the dog—both of them well aware that there was no dog—and added vegetables she had bought yesterday from the bruised bin. Tonight they'd have the meat from the bones for their dinner, and tomorrow they'd drink the soup.

This afternoon, she decided, I'll go and see the supermarket about a job again. With any luck they'll respond to a bit of tactful nagging.

She had asked a fortnight ago, and been told that there was no opening. They'd taken her name and address and said they'd contact her, but it wouldn't hurt to show her enthusiasm. Even though she knew there was no position for her. Possibly never would be.

Soon she'd be twenty-five, and it seemed as though her life had been an endless grind of work and worry and fear. Such dreams she'd had once, such hopes—all shattered.

'That,' she said aloud, 'is enough of that! Self-pity is not going to get you anywhere.' And then she began to cough, deep, barking paroxysms that shook her frame and hurt her throat and chest.

Unfortunately, telling herself that depression was the usual accompaniment to illness didn't seem to help much; she still felt oddly lackadaisical.

'I'll make Simon a new pair of trousers,' she said, using a false cheerfulness to force herself to do it. A month ago she'd bought a skirt at the op-shop which would cut up well.

Setting her lips into a firm line, she took out her old sewing machine—one which she'd earned in her wandering days. Another house-truck family owned it then, but the woman hated sewing. In return for making clothes for all the family, Olivia had been given the machine.

Normally she enjoyed the challenge of creating something new from something old, but after laying the material out on the table she put the scissors down and stared at it.

The last thing she wanted to do was sew.

Perhaps, she thought with a quick glance at the clock, she was hungry. However, the sandwich she made was so unappetising that she put it down after a couple of mouthfuls and sat at the table with her head on her arms, trying to block out the grey mist of hopelessness.

Someone knocked on the door.

A religious caller, she thought with foggy lethargy. Go away.

The knock was repeated—this time a peremptory tattoo that brought her to her feet.

Listlessly she opened the door, and to her utter astonishment there stood Drake Arundell—tall, broad-shouldered, his lean, heavily muscled body elegantly clad in a superbly tailored suit—almost blocking the narrow balcony that served as the access along the back of the flats.

On a sharp, indrawn breath she snatched the door back to shield her body, her eyes dilating endlessly as she looked up into a harshly contoured, expressionless face. Colour leached from her skin and a faint cold sweat slicked over her temples.

Quick as she was, he was quicker, and of course he was infinitely stronger. Without visibly exerting pressure he pushed the door open and walked into the room. Olivia fell back before him.

Foreboding washed through her, a hallow nausea caused by shock and dread. When her heart started up again she found it difficult to breathe.

Moving with the feline grace she remembered so well, he followed her across the room, his eyes revealing nothing but sardonic amusement. Even if she hadn't seen the forceful features she would have recognised Drake Arundell by his gait alone. After all, she had known him all her life—although it wasn't until she was fourteen and he was twenty-two that she'd noticed him with the inner eyes of her burgeoning womanhood.

He'd walked down the main street of a little town a lifetime away, and everyone in Springs Flat had watched him—some appreciatively, and some, the parents of young, impressionable daughters, with acute foreboding.

It was the sort of walk that had persuaded the elders of uncounted tribes the world over and down the centuries to look around for a war, or for big game to be hunted, or for an exploratory trip—anything to get that lean-hipped, lithely graceful saunterer out of the district and away from their wives and daughters.

Already famous, earning big money on the Formula One circuit, he was a certainty, her stepfather had said admiringly, to win the World Drivers' Championship soon.

Brian Harley used to enjoy teasing Drake's father, who worked in his accountancy firm, because Stan Arundell had resisted his son's ambitions. A conventional, hard-working man, he'd wanted Drake to take law at university, and he had used Mrs Arundell's long battle with illness to restrain his son. It had been Brian who had persuaded him to give Drake his blessing. Immediately Drake had left school, and within a remarkably few months had been racing his snarling monsters.

The situation was laden with ironic overtones; however, there was no irony in the expression of the man who was stalking her across her own room. All she could read in his face was a predatory, cold threat.

Compelled by some absurd conviction that the only way she'd retain control of the situation would be to stop retreating, Olivia came to a sudden, stubborn halt in the middle of the room, hands clenched stiffly at her sides.

He stopped too, just within her area of personal space.

Olivia's eyes travelled reluctantly to his face. At twenty-two he had been amazingly magnetic in a potent, bad-boy way that had set the fourteen-year-old Olivia's heart thumping erratically whenever her eyes had met those wicked grey-green ones. By the time she was seventeen the raffish appeal had altered to a tougher, more formidable fascination. Now time and experience had curbed and transmuted his raw intensity into a self-sufficient, hard-edged maturity.

He had always been disturbing; now he was dangerous.

Endeavouring to swallow her nervousness, she said crisply, 'Hello, Drake.'

His unwavering eyes were instantly hooded by thick black lashes. The meagre light from the central bulb splintered into red-black sparks on his hair, refracting through the light mist of rain there; devil's colouring, her mother used to say.

No, she wouldn't think of her mother now.

'Hello, Olivia.' His deep voice was abraded by an attractively rough, sensual undernote that brought a world of memories flooding back—most of them tarnished by subsequent events.

Expediency dictated a polite response. 'How are you?'

Distrusting his smile, resenting the leisurely survey that ranged the five feet six inches from her old slippers to the top of her honey-blonde head, Olivia had to suppress a swift angry reaction as he said suavely, 'Curious, as you intended me to be. Your letter was practically guaranteed to bring me at a gallop.'

'But it didn't. I wrote over a fortnight ago.'

He smiled—not a nice smile. 'I've been overseas. I came as soon as I could.'

She held out her hand, willing it not to tremble. After a taut moment his engulfed it. The brief, warm grip sent electricity up her arm and through every nerve cell in her body.

'Thank you,' she said simply, discovering that it was impossible to retrieve any composure while pinned by the steady, inimical gaze of those perceptive eyes, emotionless as quartz.

He looked around, his brows climbing as he took in the room. Stolidly Olivia suffered that unsettling scrutiny. She knew exactly what he was thinking: What on earth was Olivia Nicholls doing in a place like this?

Well, she'd done her best and she wasn't ashamed of the flat. Nevertheless she braced herself for the comment she could see coming.

'Sewing, Olivia?'

'I'm very good at it,' she said. 'Until a couple of weeks ago I was a professional seamstress.'

'What happened?'

'The factory is moving to Fiji. It's a lot cheaper to hire labour there.' Losing her job had been the final straw; that was when she'd admitted she had no hope of saving the money she needed so desperately. Until then she'd thought she might make it. She tried not to let her bitterness and fear show in her voice, but his perceptive glance revealed that she hadn't succeeded.

He continued his leisurely perusal of the room, and when she was so angry that she knew her cheeks were fiery, said evenly, 'You still look just like a cheerleader.'

'A—what?'

His mouth pulled up at the corners, but there was no amusement in his eyes. With a speculative irony that further ruffled her already shaky composure, he said, 'A cheerleader. You must have seen them on television. In America they cheer the local teams on. Long-stemmed and open and vivacious, they look healthy and nice and sexy and athletic all at once. When you were seventeen I used to think you were cheerleader material.'

No cheerleader had a pale, thin face and hair that hung lankly around her neck because she couldn't afford to get it cut.

'It must be my Anglo-Saxon genes,' she said, not hiding her resentment well enough. She hesitated, then went on without quite meeting his eyes, 'Are you married?'

'No,' he said without expression, adding with suspicious gentleness, 'But married or not, Olivia, I won't easily be blackmailed.'

She shook her head indignantly. 'That's not what I—'

Something quick and ugly behind the screen of his lashes made her inhale sharply and lose the track of her reply. Although it took all of her courage she stood her ground, holding his gaze with a lifted chin and straight back, calling on a recklessness she hadn't even known she possessed.

'I'm not actually looking for a wife at the moment, if that's what you had in mind.' His tone was insulting, as was the look that accompanied it.

Of course she didn't want to answer a slur like that, and of course the tide of colour that gave fleeting life to her pallor probably convinced him that that was exactly why she had written to him.

Since his sixteenth year Drake Arundell had been chased unmercifully—and not just by women his own age or impressionable adolescents. Now, with his potent, hard-edged appeal only slightly smoothed by superb clothes and an aura of power and sophistication, he probably had to shake women out of his sheets every night.

She was casting about for some suitable answer when he continued blandly, 'What happened, Olivia?'

A meaningless smile pulled her lips tight. 'My mother died.'

He displayed no emotion. All that could be said for him was that he was no hypocrite.

'I'm sorry to hear that,' he said distantly, the words a mere conventional expression of regret. 'Why is Elizabeth Harley's daughter, and Simon Brentshaw's granddaughter, reduced to living like this?'

'One of my grandfather's pet hobbyhorses was his belief that it was extremely bad for young people to grow up knowing they had a cushion of money behind them. He thought it corrupted them. He told me right from the start that there wouldn't be anything for me. I don't know whether he left anything to my mother, but if he did none of it was handed on to me when she died,' she said unemotionally.

He frowned. 'I see. Well, it's none of my business. Why did you write me that rather enigmatic letter?'

'Simon was just over a year old when my mother died,' she returned, leashing her anger and disillusion because she had to keep a cool head.

'And who,' he asked softly, 'is Simon?'

She tamped down incipient hysteria. 'Simon is your son.'

Astonishment glittered in the cold eyes before being banished so completely that she wondered whether she had seen aright. Oh, he was a brilliant actor! If she didn't know better, she thought bitterly, she'd believe he hadn't known of the child he'd fathered the year she was seventeen.

'Ah,' he said quietly. 'No wonder you wanted me married! Not that it would have made any difference.' His cold gaze wandered her body as he said scathingly, 'I might have kissed you when you were seventeen, Olivia, and even done a little groping, but I never took you to bed. And nowadays, fortunately for me, I can prove that he's no child of mine. If you persist with this farrago of lies I'll have your bastard DNA-tested, and then I'll prosecute you for attempted extortion.'

'Who the hell do you think you are?' she demanded, suddenly imbued with a strength she'd lacked during the past few months. 'I wouldn't have slept with you—'

'You damned near did everything but sit up and beg for it! In the end I had to tell you that I wasn't interested.'

She said in a quick, unsteady voice, 'Simon is not *my* child! You know he's my half-brother—and you're his father!'

CHAPTER TWO

A TENSE silence enfolded them both. Stealing a glance at his face, Olivia could read nothing there except a chilly contempt.

'And how do you know that?' he asked in a lethal, silky tone.

'Because my mother said so,' she retorted, masking the rapid gut-punch of fear with scorn of her own. 'She also told me that you knew about him, so it's no use trying to pretend you had no idea of his existence.'

Olivia had been in love with Drake that long-ago summer when Simon was conceived, and even after his cruel rejection of an offer she hadn't known she'd made she'd carried the memory of his kiss in some hidden, guarded place in her heart. Foolish and naïve of her, but then at seventeen surely one was allowed to be foolish and naïve about one's first love?

It had taken the revelation of Simon's parentage to destroy both. While she had been shyly, secretly falling in love with Drake, while he had been flirting with her, he had been sleeping with her mother.

Perhaps she could have forgiven him that, for Elizabeth had been radiantly beautiful, possessing a charm and sweetness that had drawn people to her all her life. But after that summer affair Drake had left them all to go to hell in their respective ways. His rejection of his son, his desertion of her mother, had set the seal on Olivia's disillusion.

Even now he was refusing to admit that he had a child. Although his features were clamped into immobility, his eyes frozen beneath half-closed lids, she could feel his rejection like a palpable force in the room.

'Start at the beginning,' he said in a voice that made her jump, 'and tell me exactly what she said.'

She hesitated, because that meant reopening scars she had hoped were healed. However, one glance told her that there was no disobeying the implacable command in his gaze. In a controlled, flat voice she said, 'Simon was born about seven months after you left Springs Flat.'

'I see. What makes you think he wasn't your stepfather's child? And don't tell me he couldn't have children. He had a daughter by his first wife. Ramona Harley left him and took her daughter back to America long before you came on the scene, but I remember her.'

Olivia looked down at her hands. 'My mother said that she hadn't slept with him for over a year,' she said tonelessly.

'She could have lied.'

Her head moved in sharp denial. 'No. That's what they were quarrelling about—he knew Simon wasn't his.'

For all the interest he showed she might have been reciting her times tables. 'How did your mother die?'

She turned her head away from those intimidating eyes. 'She—she fell one night and hit her head on the corner of the table.'

'So how did that lead to her daughter ending up in a place like this with her half-brother? Your stepfather is still alive, I believe.'

'Yes.' Shocked by the whispering feebleness of her reply, she stiffened her spine. Damn him, he had no right to interrogate her as though she were on the witness stand! 'He—was unkind to Simon, so after my mother was—died—I took Simon away.'

His brows drew together. Astute eyes scanned her face in a merciless, unhurried survey. 'And he let you go?

Just like that? A seventeen—no, you'd have been eighteen—'

'Does it matter?' She glowered down at her hands, so tightly clasped that the knuckles were white. Her body language, she thought mordantly, couldn't have been more explicit. Carefully she loosened her grip. He noticed, of course, those narrowed eyes following the betraying little movement.

Swiftly, defiantly, she said, 'I was nineteen, actually. But however old I was, Simon is your son! As you'll discover when you have him DNA-tested.' She tried to hide the disdain in her tone, but feared she'd made a bad fist of it.

Although his eyes rested on her face with insulting indifference, she was sure that she could hear the smooth meshing of gears as his brain sorted out the information he needed. When he spoke she almost jumped again.

'Tell me why you left your stepfather. And this time no rubbish about him not liking the child. I want the truth.'

Every muscle in her body tensed, but because she had rehearsed the answer the words came easily. 'He resented Simon. I was afraid he'd hurt him.'

She held her breath, letting it out in a small huff of surprise when he demanded no further explanations. 'All right,' he said slowly. 'Why have you waited until now to contact me?'

'You made it very obvious you didn't want anything to do with either my mother or your son. Anyway, I didn't know where you were. After your accident you dropped out of sight completely.'

'So how did you find out where I was?'

She set her teeth. 'I saw your photo in the paper.'

'And you thought, Aha, here's a pigeon ripe for the plucking—'

'No! Simon has glue ear, damn you. Do you know what that means? He's going deaf, and he can't hear the teacher—can't understand what she's telling him, or the sounds she's trying to teach him in reading. He needs grommets put into his eardrums to drain the ears and every day he waits he drops a little further behind at school.

'They didn't pick it up until he'd been at school for a year, so he's already lost a lot of ground. His behaviour is getting worse too. He used to love school, but now he hates it because the other kids say he's stupid and call him a dummy. He gets into fights and is disruptive, simply because he can't hear and can't keep up. The waiting list to have grommets put in is over a year, and I can't afford to get it done privately.'

She knew she should tone her aggression down, sound moderate and demure and appealing, but when she thought of Simon's bewildered suffering during the past year it was all she could do not to swear and shout and throw a tantrum.

'Your devotion to the child is exemplary.' He was watching her, his hard mouth compressed into a straight line, grey-green eyes opaque and unmoved. When he continued it was with unnerving precision. 'But you've chosen the wrong man, Olivia. I'm not so conveniently weak I'd let you foist your child on me.'

He is not my child. Taking in a deep breath, she unclenched her tight jaw and said pleadingly, 'Drake, please. You can't turn away from your own son!'

'You're right,' he agreed calmly. 'I wouldn't turn away from my own son. It was a nice try, Olivia, but you went about it the wrong way. If you'd written the usual begging letter I might have helped for old times' sake.' His eyes wandered openly down her body, returned with cool, speculative contempt to her pale face. 'I don't blackmail easily.'

Desperation drove her to say fiercely, 'If you won't help him I'll go to the newspapers and tell them—'

His hands snaked out, catching her wrists in a grip so strong that she winced and cried out. Long fingers relaxing slightly, he said with a soft sibilance that was infinitely more frightening than a loud bluster could ever have been, 'Stop right now.'

The tumultuous words died on her tongue. She dragged in a shaky breath, suddenly aware that she didn't really know this man, that they were alone and she was weakened by illness.

Gripped by a sickening fear that she might have done something so irrevocable that all their lives would be marked by it, Olivia's senses were on full alert; the skin across the back of her neck prickled and tightened, made preternaturally sensitive by her acute awareness of Drake Arundell's fingers around her wrists. Shocked, she realised that she could smell him—a faint, infinitely troubling scent that set her nerve ends tingling.

Fight or flee, she thought, trying to calm the violent beating of her heart. She couldn't flee, and intuition warned her that she risked more than she understood if she fought; no wonder tension iced her stomach and clouded her brain.

And then she heard Simon's voice. 'Liv!' he shouted, clattering up the outside staircase. 'Hey, Liv, guess what? There's a cool Jag outside! I wonder...'

No! I'm not ready for this! Olivia thought feverishly, wrenching her hands free. Bending so that her face couldn't be seen, she pretended to pick up a piece of thread from the floor, only straightening when Simon came tearing into the room, honey-gold hair tossing in the wind of his progress, golden-brown eyes sparkling with unaccustomed vitality.

'...whose it is!' he finished, skidding to a halt as he took in the tableau in front of him.

'What are you doing home?' she asked too sharply. 'School hasn't finished yet.'

'Yes, it has so.' He flushed, jutting his bottom lip.

Not now! she thought. He had gone through the 'terrible twos' with no sign of tantrums, but since his hearing had deteriorated they came frequently.

He thought better of it this time, though. 'We had a concert and then they sent us home,' he said, directing sideways looks at the man who was watching him impassively.

Later she'd make sure Simon hadn't bunked school, but at that moment all she could say was, 'This is Mr Arundell, Simon.'

'Hello,' Simon said, suddenly wary as a half-grown wolf cub. 'I'm Simon Harley.' He advanced into the room and looked uncertainly at Olivia.

Drake said, 'How do you do, Simon?' and held out his hand.

Cautiously Simon shook it. 'How do you do?' he replied, staring up in awe. 'Is that your car down there?'

Olivia looked from the smooth childish features to the guarded face of the man who had just repudiated his son, and wondered whether she could see some resemblance.

No, none. Like her, Simon bore Elizabeth's stamp.

And yet... An elusive tingle of memory teased her mind before escaping into oblivion.

'It is,' Drake Arundell said, all grey leached from eyes that were now pure green.

Olivia said quietly, 'Darling, go and wash your hands—they're filthy.'

'What?'

She repeated the command in the clear, slightly nasal tone that seemed to get through best to him.

'OK.'

He gave a respectful smile to Drake Arundell, who waited until the door into the bathroom had closed firmly behind him before saying in a low, level voice, 'You can't even claim he looks like me. He's—'

In an equally muted voice Olivia interrupted, 'We can't talk now.'

His head came up as though she had struck him on the jaw. Inwardly quailing at the icy lack of emotion in his eyes, Olivia refused to back down; she stared him directly in the face, silently forbidding him to upset the child who was noisily splashing water over his hands in the bathroom.

'We aren't going to talk at all,' he said curtly. 'I fight dirty, Olivia. If you annoy me any more I'll find a painful way to clip your claws.' He swung around and strode out, long legs moving fast, the set of his broad shoulders and the way he held his head expressing anger and contempt.

Olivia's breath hissed through her lips. She stood listening to the sounds of the neighbourhood, so familiar that for years she had barely heard them. Cars changed gear and swung around the corner, impatient brakes screeching on the wet tarseal. A siren wailed down the motorway, its imperative command only slightly muted by the houses between.

Her stomach felt as though it had been kicked by a rugby forward. Even though she had rehearsed their meeting ever since posting the letter, she hadn't been prepared.

But then, nothing would have prepared her for this version of Drake Arundell.

He's not going to get away with it, she thought fiercely. I'll find a way...

'Oh, he's gone?' Simon appeared at the bathroom door. Somehow the statement came out as a question heavily underlined with disappointment.

'Yes.' Olivia walked across to the sink, drew a glass of water and drank it down.

'Who is he?'

Although she'd also rehearsed a couple of answers to that question, now that it had been asked neither seemed appropriate. 'Someone I knew when I was seventeen,' she said lightly, hoping that it didn't sound too evasive.

Simon nodded, but she hadn't stifled his curiosity. They had very few visitors, and none who drove Jaguar cars. 'Is he coming back?'

'Possibly,' she said vaguely, setting the glass down. 'Make yourself a sandwich, darling, and then I'll hear you read.'

He pulled a face, but he knew the rules. At least, she thought wearily, she didn't have to worry about television's influence on him; they didn't have a set. As he was beginning to point out more and more frequently.

Simon was clever and quick, but in spite of all her efforts he was rapidly losing ground. Olivia was determined that he should have his chance; he wasn't going to be sentenced to a life like hers, held back by circumstances.

Facing down Drake Arundell was a small price to pay, and why should he refuse to accept his responsibilities when so far he'd got off scot-free?

Later, as she prepared dinner, she tried to work out another plan of campaign for dealing with the man. She hadn't expected him to be so—so intimidating, she decided after searching for the word. However, it was too late to worry about that now. If he refused to take a DNA test she'd simply raise such a fuss that he'd have to.

After they'd eaten and done the dishes she dragged out the cheap writing pad and a pen.

'What are you doing?'

'Writing a letter,' she said casually.

Simon's eyes rounded. They never wrote letters—or got them for that matter. 'Who to?' he asked with a guarded curiosity that hurt. A year ago he'd have been filled with eager interest.

'A man,' she said, narrowing her eyes mysteriously as she dropped her voice to a significant whisper. 'And I'm not going to tell you who he is—you'll just have to wait.'

Grinning, he left her to it, sitting on the sofa which was also her bed to 'read' a school library book. Listening to him stumble over words, she thought wearily that these first years at school were vital. If he lost too much ground it could take him years to catch up. And he might become so convinced of his inferiority that he'd never make up the gap.

She finished the letter. But although she had made it much more emphatic, she read it with a furrowed brow. There was nothing in it to stop Drake dismissing it with a flick of those lean, strong fingers.

Absently she touched the place on one wrist where he'd held her fast. He hadn't hurt her, but she'd known she wasn't going to be able to escape that grip. A frisson of sensation shivered across her nerves, heating them with a forbidden fire.

What would he be like as a lover?

Immediately the dreamy sensuality was replaced by shocked indignation. No doubt her mother had shivered to the same deliciously sinful sensation, asked herself the same wicked question. But Elizabeth Harley had found the answer—and the knowledge had cost her happiness and peace of mind, and ultimately her life.

Look at it whichever way you liked, Drake owed Simon, and it was time that he did something about it.

Setting her jaw, Olivia tore up the letter and wrote another.

Dear Drake,
I'm sure you wouldn't like to appear on the cover of something like this. I'll contact this one if that's the only way I can find the money for Simon's operation.

Tomorrow she'd buy an old copy of one of those magazines from the secondhand book shop at the end of the row opposite. Drake would discover that she could fight dirty too, when it was necessary.

The next morning she and Simon went off to school, where she discovered that he had been telling the truth about his early arrival home. Only then admitting to herself how afraid she had been that he'd bunked, she returned home with a marginally lighter heart.

On the way, still inflamed with fury and righteousness, she bought a magazine with the most outrageous and embarrassing headline she could find, tore off the cover, folded it into four and stuffed it into the envelope with her letter, then posted it.

Scarcely two hours after the mailman had collected the mail from the box outside the dairy she realised that Drake could quite easily contact her stepfather and tell him where she was.

At first such terror enveloped her that she collapsed into a chair, her stomach quivering with panic, her mouth moving as she said aloud, 'He wouldn't—surely?'

Of course he wouldn't.

No one, not even a man who had repudiated his son, would willingly put a child in jeopardy.

Not even Drake Arundell.

But although she tried to reassure herself, she couldn't. The loss of her job meant that her days, once busy to the point of bursting, were now long and too full of empty hours—hours in which she could spin fantasies of Simon being torn from her arms by a vengeful Brian Harley. She even went so far as to get all their clothes out onto Simon's bed and make them into parcels in case they had to flee from the flat.

Reason prevailed and she put them away, but she began to look nervously about her, seeing a threat in every stranger.

There followed two of the most worrying days of her life. In the evening of the third day after she'd sent the letter the knock she'd been expecting came. Swallowing, deliberately steadying her voice, she said, 'Yes, who is it?'

'Open the door, Olivia.'

Wiping suddenly damp palms down her thighs, Olivia did as she was told. Cool, clammy air rushed into the flat, its petrol-scented breath evocative of too many people trying to get home through the rain. Drake loomed in the entrance, yet it wasn't so much his size that disturbed her as that mysterious thing called presence. Drake had too much, and in his case it was spiced with enough danger to impress even the most foolhardy.

Her eyes flicked across to the child who had curled up on the old sofa-bed and fallen asleep with the unexpectedness of childhood. It was too late now to turn back. All she could hope was that she didn't show just how nervous she was; Drake would pick up any signs and use them to his advantage.

'Come in,' she said quietly.

He looked around, once more taking in the landlord's cheap furniture, the total lack of anything that looked as though money had been spent on it. His eyes came to rest on Simon, snuggled under the blanket Olivia had draped over him. He frowned. 'Is that where he sleeps?'

'No,' she said evenly. 'He has a bed in the bedroom.'

'With you?'

Biting off the words, she retorted, 'I sleep out here on the sofa-bed.'

Astonishingly he said, 'The last time I saw you, you were seventeen years old, gleaming golden with the gloss that money and confidence and a good school gave you. Your stepfather was the town's only accountant—and comparatively rich—and you intended to go to university and become a lawyer. You've come a long way from there.'

She pressed her lips together.

He said impatiently, 'You can tell me about it tomorrow morning at eleven in my office.'

'I can't come in to your office—' she began, indignation edging the words.

'Keep your voice down. You'll wake the boy.'

'His name is Simon, and he won't wake.'

'It makes no difference what his name is,' he returned curtly. Reaching into his pocket, he took out a wallet and opened it, removing a card. 'Eleven tomorrow morning,' he reiterated, setting it down on the table. 'Make sure you're on time. If you don't turn up, Olivia, the next person on your doorstep will be a policeman with a warrant for attempted extortion. That second letter was not a good move.'

He turned and went down the stairs, moving swiftly and gracefully. Shivering, Olivia switched off the inside light and walked out to the edge of the balcony.

His car was parked in the light of a streetlamp. As she watched he opened the door and got in beside a woman clad in some crimson material. Blonde hair gleamed like satin as she turned a smiling face away from Olivia. Then the car door closed behind Drake and the internal light blinked out.

Shaken, Olivia turned and went back inside.

The next day was fine, one of those brilliant days when the sky was a cool, polished blue so deep that it seemed like a lapis-lazuli bowl inverted over the city. After leaving Simon at school, Olivia set off to walk as far as she could into Auckland before exhaustion forced her to catch a bus.

Five minutes early, she presented herself outside Drake's office in Grafton, her feelings raw with outrage, her head held so high that her shoulders ached. The building was an elegant block guarded by security men and glossy receptionists, all of whom looked at her with variations of the same smug astonishment.

She knew why Drake had insisted she come here. He'd wanted to intimidate her. And after she'd trekked over an acre or so of slippery marble she had to admit that he had succeeded.

'This way, please,' murmured his secretary, a rather large but superbly groomed woman of middle age, as she headed off across more expensive flooring, this time a carpet whose close velvet pile made Olivia's hot, tired feet curl.

Seated behind a huge, dark wooden desk, Drake was checking through a sheaf of papers. He got to his feet and said, 'Thank you, Maria.' After a narrow-eyed scrutiny of Olivia he added, 'Bring a tray, please, with something to eat.'

When the door had closed with an expensive lack of noise behind the woman, he said, 'Sit down, you look worn out.' He waited until she'd obeyed before resuming his seat behind the desk.

'I am,' she snapped, furious with him for making her come all the way here.

That unpleasant smile curled his mouth. 'Bad night, Olivia?'

'Not particularly,' she lied, wondering what he'd say if he ever found out that her sleeplessness had been caused more by the glimpse of the woman beside him than by his threats.

He'd probably laugh; he'd certainly use such knowledge against her.

Her letter and the torn cover of the magazine were in front of him, a jarring, tawdry note in that expensive, restrained room. Drake's lean, tanned forefinger didn't quite touch the cheap sheet of writing paper. He said, 'You have nerve, Olivia, but extortion is a serious crime. And I'm starting to get just a bit sick and tired of this harassment. Push me any further, and I'll see you in gaol.'

He meant it too. Olivia knew that she'd let her anger override common sense, but she couldn't back down now. She looked at him steadily.

'If that's all you wanted me to come in for, you've wasted both my time and yours,' she said, making no attempt to hide her disdain as she got to her feet. 'I despise men who think they have some macho right to get women pregnant and then abandon them. Simon needs your help now more than he'll probably ever need it again. If you never do anything else for him, you can do this. You had your chances; you had loving parents who did their best for you. Simon only has me.'

'Sit down,' he said without any inflection.

She shook her head.

'Sit down, Olivia, or I'll call the police right here and now.'

She looked into eyes so lacking in anything but an inflexible determination that they froze her right through to her soul. With an enormous reluctance—and only, she told herself, because she was so tired—she sank back into the chair.

'And if I do this for him,' he said coldly, 'what will you want the money for next time? Because black-mailers never stop, Olivia. Even when they believe their reasons for extorting the money are impeccably moral.'

Maria came in with a tray, setting it down in front of Olivia.

'Thank you,' Drake said, waiting until the older woman had left the room before commanding, 'Pour yourself a cup of tea. And eat something, for heaven's sake. You look like death.'

'I'll just have milk,' she said. 'I don't drink coffee or tea.'

'Still?' His smile was thin and too perceptive. When she had poured a cup of milk he resumed, 'Go on, have a sandwich. They're very good.'

'How do you know?' They looked delicious, but pride forbade her to eat anything that he'd paid for.

He laughed softly. 'I quite often have them for lunch.'

Hoping sourly that one day he'd understand how lucky he was to be able to afford them, Olivia drank some milk. The cool liquid slid down her throat, but instead of soothing the rawness it inflamed it. She took a deep breath and had to hold it to stop an incipient cough; when she finally breathed out, her chest wheezed faintly. Hoping that it wasn't too audible, she took another sip of milk. She didn't want to betray any weakness at all— not even physically.

'All right,' Drake said calmly, 'exactly how did you come to be looking after Simon? Why didn't you go on to university as you planned?'

She finished the milk and looked down at her hands. The sandwiches intruded into her line of sight. Firmly ignoring their seductive appeal, she said with enormous reluctance, 'I couldn't leave my mother.'

'Why not?'

'She—relied on me. She needed me. She was ill.'

It told the relevant details; it hid so much more.

Eyes the wind-driven grey of an arctic sea scanned her face. 'Your mother told you that I was the boy's father?'

'No,' she said stiffly, holding herself erect. 'I over-heard her tell my stepfather.'

Drake's eyes were fastened on hers, as though he could chisel out the truth by merely looking at her.

She had washed her hair and put on lipstick for this interview, and something had driven her to don her one reasonably good skirt and blouse and put up her hair in a French knot. Disgust at the realisation that she was primping for him had made her brush her hair out of the knot so briskly that tears had stung her eyes, and tether the long locks into their usual ponytail.

When he spoke it was in a voice that was cool and dispassionate. Yet she sensed steel beneath the judicial words—the leashed strength of emotions held rigidly in check.

'You seem to do a lot of overhearing. Why are you so convinced that your mother was telling the truth about Simon's father?'

'Because she was my mother,' she retorted, angry at the slur on her behaviour. She had overheard one quarrel of many. 'Don't you believe your mother?'

He gave her a sardonic look. 'I'd believe my mother if she said I was born an alien on Mars—but then, she has an obsession with the truth. I've never known her to perpetrate even a white lie, whereas your mother had a fund of pleasantries she didn't expect her listeners to believe. How did your stepfather react when your mother flung this bombshell at him?'

'How would you react?' she asked bleakly, hating him for his merciless assessment of Elizabeth Harley—an assessment that was, alas, almost true. Her mother had been a superb hostess, eager to make sure that everyone enjoyed themselves in her home. Sometimes that had meant she'd welcomed people she'd disliked. Yet her sincerity had never seemed forced.

'Badly,' he said.

A note in his voice sent a shiver chasing across Olivia's skin. Brian Harley had shouted and blustered and hit her mother with his clenched fist at least once before Olivia had rushed into the room, but at this moment she was more afraid of Drake Arundell than she had ever been of her stepfather.

Contempt cut through the slight roughness of his voice. 'I wonder why she hated me so much.'

Fire gleamed beneath Olivia's dark lashes. 'Perhaps because you abandoned her,' she said between her teeth. 'You left her to my stepfather's tender mercies—'

'Why the hell did she stay?' he interrupted, looking at her with an oblique, shuttered watchfulness. 'Why didn't she go home to her father?'

Olivia had asked herself the same question a hundred times. But when Drake had abandoned her something had gone out of Elizabeth Harley; it had been as though she'd embraced her life with her husband as a penance.

Shaking her head, Olivia said, 'My grandfather was ill—he died a couple of months after Simon was born. I don't know why she stayed at Springs Flat. She just—withered away, lost the will to live.'

'So what made you run? And the truth this time.'

She sent him a fleeting glance. There was no softness in his face, nothing that gave her any hope that she might be able to fool him.

'I think my stepfather killed her,' she said baldly. 'And I was afraid he would kill Simon.'

The words resounded with ugly significance in the spacious, elegant room. The last time she'd said them had been when she'd asked for refuge with her best friend in Wellington.

She had expected to shock him, but no muscle moved in the harsh, austere face. 'What makes you think he killed Elizabeth?' he asked.

'Two nights before she died he—he came home slightly drunk; I wanted to stay up, but my mother made me go to bed. I heard them quarrelling downstairs and then she came up alone. She was crying and I didn't go into her—she hated me to see her cry. In the morning I found her unconscious on the floor. She died a couple of days later. At the post mortem it was decided that she'd fallen and hit her head on the bedside table.'

'You didn't tell anyone about the quarrel?'

She said, 'No. I didn't think then that he'd killed her, otherwise I would have. And the doctor said that although the blow had been enough to send her into a coma, he was surprised that it had been bad enough to kill her.'

'But—?' he prompted.

She swallowed and drank a little more of the milk. 'After the inquest I cleaned up her bedroom and found his tie—the one he'd worn that night—curled up under the bed. I remembered he'd had it on that night because it was his school tie. So I knew he'd been in her room.'

'There are a hundred different reasons why he could have taken his tie off in her room,' Drake said.

'Not the way things were with them,' she said, knowing that it was hopeless, but compelled to continue.

Her belief in her stepfather's viciousness was based on much more subtle evidence than the brutal results of a blow, or a tie in the wrong place. But a look, an expression, wouldn't stand up in a court of law. And it wouldn't convince Drake.

Nevertheless, she had to try. 'Anyway—about a fortnight after the funeral, I went in to check on Simon, and my—stepfather—he—' She stopped, her throat working as she tried to get the words out.

'Go on,' Drake said mercilessly.

She looked down at the hands writhing in her lap. It took considerable expenditure of willpower to stop their involuntary movement.

In a remote, brittle voice she said, 'He was standing by the cot with a pillow in his hands. I said, "Was he restless?" And he said, "Yes. I thought he might like a pillow." But Simon was never restless; he slept like a log every night. He still does. And there was a look in my stepfather's face... I knew he didn't like Simon, but I never knew he hated him. A little boy, and he hated him...' With an effort she kept her voice steady. 'So I took him and ran away.'

'Did he follow you?'

She shivered. 'I don't know.'

'Where did you go?'

'To a friend—my best friend from school. She was going to Victoria University. In Wellington.'

'I know where Victoria is,' he said, smiling lethally. 'I didn't go to university myself, but I do read newspapers. And some of my best friends graduated from Victoria.'

'Yes, well,' she said, feeling exactly the way he wanted her to—as though she'd tried to patronise him. 'Emma has a brother, Neil. He was there that night. They didn't believe me at first, but Emma knows me; she knew I wouldn't lie. So she suggested that I hide in Neil's housetruck with Simon while we went across Cook Strait on the ferry. That way my stepfather wouldn't know we'd left the North Island.'

'Where did you go then?'

'I decided to stay with Neil,' she said. 'He wanted someone to look after the house and cook meals while he made jewellery.'

It had worked perfectly. For two years she and Simon had wandered with Neil, a kind, gentle man who had made no demands on her. He'd taught her how to cook and she'd earned a frugal living by picking fruit and doing other seasonal jobs. Gradually she learned how to survive legally in a world where she couldn't risk claiming any benefit other than unemployment for fear of having Simon returned to the man who hated him.

'And what ended this idyll?'

She flashed him a suspicious glance, but he looked merely a little bored. 'Neil wanted to go to Australia,' she said stiffly. 'I couldn't go—I didn't dare get Simon a passport.'

And she had longed for a settled home. Here, in New Zealand's biggest city, she'd been sure they'd be safe. The flat had been her dingy little haven.

'I see,' he said, giving nothing away. 'So you've been here—how long?'

'Three years.'

Winged black brows lifted. 'And clearly things are not going well for you.'

'We've managed until now.' She endeavoured not to sound defensive.

His smile was cold and cruel and pitiless as he homed in on her weak spot. 'Tell me, Olivia, why did you wait for—it must be eight years, surely, since we saw each other last?'

'Seven,' she said, controlling a sudden, baseless fear with an effort.

'I'm flattered you remember so accurately.'

'It's not difficult,' she said, unable to hide a note of bitterness, although she managed to keep her expression composed. His departure had marked the beginning of the end of her world.

'So why didn't you try to contact me five years ago, when you ran away, your babe in your arms in the traditional manner?'

She met the bland enquiry of his gaze with something close to anger. Clearly he wasn't going to make this easy, but Simon's future was at stake—and for Simon she would put up with this barely hidden insolence.

Bluntly she said, 'I've already told you. By then you'd gone into hiding after your accident, and anyway I never planned to contact you. But he needs to have his ears done straight away. And you owe him a future, Drake.'

He watched her with half-closed eyes in which all trace of green had been swallowed by an icy grey. 'You must have known of this rather minor condition of his for some years.'

'It is not minor!' she flared. 'Already Simon's starting to get bored because he can't really hear what the teacher is saying. How well would you have done at school if you'd heard everything as though you were six feet under water? His behaviour is deteriorating. These first few years of school are vitally important—'

'You've already had a go at wringing my heart with this spiel,' he interrupted, the languid tones sharpened now by an edge of steel. 'Why now, Olivia? Why not five years ago, when your mother died? Why not when you found out about his ears? I want the truth.'

'Five years ago you were swanning around race tracks enjoying yourself by spraying huge bottles of champagne over anyone who'd stand still for it.'

'I got hurt the season Simon was born,' he said, deflating her righteous indignation.

'Yes, well, I didn't contact you because I was certain you'd deny it, and I didn't know there was a way of forcing you to admit paternity,' she said, not trying to hide her contempt, even though common sense screamed that she should not antagonise him further. 'But when I read about the DNA test I knew I could make it stick.'

'Is that the only reason?'

She stared at him, meeting eyes that were cold and pitiless. Something moved in her stomach—a clutch of genuine fear. Slowly she shook her head.

How could a mouth like his—sexy, sensually sculptured—smile so unpleasantly? 'When were you going to tell me that you need two thousand dollars, Olivia?' he asked silkily.

Bitterly ashamed, she said, 'I only want to borrow it...'

'I'm sure. Tell me how you wound up owing two thousand dollars.'

'Simon woke up one night with abscesses on his eardrums. I borrowed my next-door neighbour's car—he was too drunk to drive, but he said it would be all right to use it to take Simon to the hospital. It would have been too, only someone hit me on a roundabout, and neither car had insurance. Brett's car was totalled.'

She shivered. It amazed her that neither she nor Simon—nor the driver of the other car—had suffered more than a few cuts and bruises when both cars had been completely demolished. 'I owe him that money,' she finished, adding lamely, 'How did you know about it?'

'I had you investigated.'

She sent him a furious, frustrated glance, but said nothing.

He was smiling. 'Your neighbour thinks you're a nice kid—a bit repressed, but with a heart in the right place. He seems remarkably casual about the whole affair.'

'He's a dear,' she said. 'Very laid back.'

Brett knew that she couldn't afford to pay him the value of his car, so he'd written it off without any complaints or irritation.

'How close a friend is he?'

'He's not a friend, just a neighbour.' And then she realised what he was implying. Her eyes flashed gold fire as she returned arrogantly, 'Your investigator can't be very good if he hasn't discovered that.'

She expected Drake to say more, but to her astonishment he left the subject of her enormous debt and asked levelly, 'How do you plan to persuade me to take a DNA test? I don't imagine you can pay the twelve hundred or so dollars it's going to cost. Or the lawyer's fees.'

Why should she get the heart-chilling impression that there was nothing more he wanted to do than to squeeze the life out of her? She had had enough of this cat-and-mouse business.

Taking a deep, calming breath, she lifted her chin and retorted, 'No. If you don't give me some money for Simon's ears I'll take you to court—and married or not it's going to look bad, especially when it turns out that you *are* his father. You don't have to give me it all— I've got almost three hundred dollars saved up.'

'We have yet to ascertain exactly whose child he is.' Long, tanned fingers suddenly moved on the arms of the chair, then were stilled. His deliberate scrutiny stripped the outer layers of her defences away; afraid that he could see the terrified child who hid at her innermost core, she blinked.

At last he said abruptly, 'All right, we'll get it done. You, me and Simon. I'll pay.'

CHAPTER THREE

IMMEDIATELY after the momentary flash of elation came suspicion. Why? Not even when she'd assumed he was married, and therefore less likely to want publicity, had she expected it to be so easy to persuade him. 'Why me?' she asked ungrammatically.

'If you won't co-operate,' he said with dispassionate indifference, 'you can forget any hope you might have of getting me to have it done. It's no use threatening to sell your story to cheap magazines with ever-open chequebooks either, because if you do that, your biggest fear will come true.'

He smiled at her blank face. 'Your stepfather will know where you are,' he supplied brutally. 'And as you'll be embroiled in a nasty court case with me, you won't be able to keep your half-brother from his evil clutches.'

She couldn't see the expression in his eyes because his lashes shielded them, but the smile that curled his beautifully cut mouth as he countered her threat sent icy splinters down the length of her spine.

'I despise you,' she said harshly, getting to her feet. For a nauseating moment her head swam, but she was defiantly glad that she hadn't eaten any of the food.

'But you'll take my money,' he said.

'He's your son, damn you! Someone has to take care of him!'

'*If* he's my son, I will,' he said coolly. 'But only him. I'm not giving you an entrée into Easy Street.'

Her mouth dropped. Although that unnerving smile still lingered, beneath his lashes she could see an unsparing determination.

48

'I don't want your wretched money for myself,' she said fiercely.

He stood up, covered the distance separating them in one stride, and stopped her instinctive retreat with a hard grip on her shoulders. Desperate, she tried to twist away, only succeeding in losing her balance.

Damn, she wailed silently as his fingers bit into her upper arms, holding her upright. Damn this wretched cold!

'Be still,' he commanded. His voice dropped. 'Now, you listen to me, Olivia Nicholls—and listen well, because this is the last time I'll say this. I'm not your ticket to the sort of life you left behind when you ran away from home.'

'I know that,' she retorted haughtily, narrowing her eyes to meet the blazing green of his.

'Just so long as you do,' he said. The anger suddenly faded from his eyes, from his face. In a voice that was deep and amused, almost companionable, he went on, 'But we both know that he's not really my child, don't we? You don't really need to go through all this business of blood tests, Olivia. I'm sure we can come to an arrangement that's convenient for both of us without involving the law.'

The conversation had assumed a tipsy, surreal aspect. Olivia felt as though she'd been lured into a fairground house of mirrors and was trapped there in a maze of irrationality, until she realised that he was merely attacking on a different front. After all, if she didn't insist on the genetic testing there'd be no proof. Staring up into the mockery of his smiling face, she searched for words.

The long walk combined with the effects of her chest cold finally caught up with her. The room began to shimmer, and then to whirl nauseatingly. Dazzled by the silver lights in his eyes, she clutched his arms and fought for control, but her knees buckled.

He made an impeded noise in the back of his throat and kissed her.

Olivia thought she had forgotten that a man's mouth could be violent and wildly exciting at the same time, but the touch of his mouth on hers showed her how wrong she was. In spite of its aftermath, the one kiss he had given her was engraved on her heart, and those long-hidden memories formed the basis of her present reaction.

He kissed her with a slow, elemental expertise. Instead of resisting, she succumbed to the consuming flood of sensation that raged out of nowhere. Drowning in its hot, sweet torrent, for long, dangerous minutes she was unable to call up the common sense and pragmatism she'd developed over the intervening years.

Overwhelmed, she yielded the tender promise of her mouth to Drake's worldly domination. As his arms contracted about her Olivia's subliminal senses picked up the signs of his response to her unguarded passion. His heartbeat began to speed up, the muscles in the big, lithe body tightened, his mouth curved in a narrow, mirthless smile, and when he lifted his head fire smouldered in his heavy-lidded eyes.

'So,' he said softly, his breath heating the acutely sensitised skin of her lips, 'some things haven't changed at all.'

It was then that she realised just exactly what he was doing. Furious, she jerked her head sideways and tried to pull away. 'Wait a minute,' she snapped. 'You've got it all wrong.'

'Really?' he murmured, obviously not at all affected by the frank eroticism of the kiss. He waited until she had stopped struggling before letting her go, and then watched her with cold-blooded speculation.

Her stomach churning, Olivia closed her eyes. The fall from mindless rapture to fury and disgust had come too quickly for her composure. 'You are utterly foul!' she snarled.

He was unreachable—made of ice, made of iron. 'Did you really think I'd be so easy to fool, Olivia, with a few heart-rending and quite unprovable stories?'

'I am not trying to con you,' she returned, aching with bitter disillusionment. Not that she should be surprised. That was all this man seemed to leave behind him. 'You're the con artist, and I'm really looking forward to seeing you admit it when the DNA test proves that Simon's your son.'

He didn't appear at all impressed by her anger. 'Or not, as the case may be. I'll organise it.'

'Right,' she said between her teeth. 'You do that small thing, Mr Arundell. Contact me when you've made the arrangements.'

She swung around and headed for the door, but as she got there she staggered again, this time saving herself from falling by a frantic clutch at the handle.

'What's the matter with you?' he demanded.

'I'm all right.' But when she tried to turn the handle her fingers wouldn't obey her, and to her horror everything in her field of vision began once more to sway ominously.

So intent was she on staying upright that she didn't know he'd moved until he caught her around the waist and pulled her back against his hard warmth. His arms were very strong, and for a perilous moment she wanted nothing more than to let herself collapse into them and give up completely.

Only for a moment, however. 'Let me go.'

'I'll take you home,' he said impatiently.

'No!'

'Olivia, don't be an idiot. I'm not going to drive you to the nearest police station, however much you deserve it. Maria, come here!'

Ten minutes later she was sitting in the leathered opulence of his car in silence, watching the lunchtime traffic go by. Ignoring her objections, he had swept her into his private lift and then into his car in the basement parking area.

They were almost back at the flat when he asked in a deceptively bland voice, 'Why are you so convinced the child is mine? And don't tell me that you believed your mother. Loving mothers have lied for a variety of good reasons before today.'

'I *know* he's yours, Mr Arundell,' she bit out.

He looked keenly at her, but said nothing beyond, 'It's too late to pretend we don't know each other well. After all, if this test shows that I'm the father of your half-brother, we're very closely connected. So you can't keep me at a distance by calling me Mr Arundell.'

For some reason she felt a searing pang of disappointment. Tracking it down to its source, she discovered that it was because he was at last admitting that he'd had an affair with her mother. And that was really ridiculous, because she had always known. A shiver ran down her spine as snatches of memories poured back: angry, raised voices, the sound of a blow, her mother's dreadful weeping...

And the corrosive, ever-present sense of betrayal that she'd experienced ever since she'd learnt who Simon's father really was.

Silly of her, because she'd had no claims on Drake. Even at seventeen she'd known that the kiss he'd given her had meant nothing to him.

Dragging her mind back to the present, she asked distantly, 'When you are suitably convinced that he is yours, what do you plan to do?'

'I think the first thing to establish is what *you* plan to do, don't you?' The deep, self-contained voice had a subtle edge to it.

His kiss had tilted her equilibrium, scrambling her thought processes into turmoil and confusion. She muttered, 'To be honest, I hadn't thought. I realise that you have a greater claim on him than I...' She swallowed, and couldn't go on.

He lifted his brow.

Hating him for making her plead, she tried for a crisp note. 'He's like my own child. And once the test is done, there's nothing my father can do about claiming him, is there?'

'I don't know what the legal position would be,' he said coolly. 'Am I to gather that you want to stay in that appalling flat with him?'

'No!'

'I thought not,' he said. 'Somewhere much nicer, perhaps? With a hefty allowance? And the two thousand dollars you owe paid off, so that you start with a clean slate?'

She said rigidly, 'No.'

'If he is my son, he'll live with me.' His voice was perfectly level, but beneath the steady tone the whip flicked, stinging.

Panic-stricken, Olivia stared at him. This was a development she hadn't anticipated. 'Why?' she demanded. 'You don't want him—you never have.'

'You must think I'm an easy target,' he said with inauspicious gentleness. 'Did you really believe, Olivia, that I would be content to pay out for a child yet have nothing to say about his upbringing?'

Put like that, it did seem foolish. 'Why now?' she asked. 'You've always known about him, but you never made any effort to contact Mother or me.'

He paused, but instead of answering her question he observed negligently, 'Who would have thought, seven years ago, that we would meet again like this?'

No trace of emotion coloured his voice, but she shrank back at the hidden undertones, the raw anger that blazed through him like fire hidden in the heart of a volcano. It both surprised and alarmed her. Surely he'd realised that embarking on an affair with a much older woman guaranteed that any subsequent meeting with her daughter would be difficult?

'Who, indeed?' she said sarcastically.

His devil's eyebrows lifted. 'I've never had anyone try to blackmail me before,' he said calmly, drawing in to the kerb beneath the flats. He gave her a long, dispassionate look, his expression aloof.

Olivia met his eyes as best she could, but an unnerving hollowness in her stomach made her feel slightly peculiar. Numbly she shook her head.

His smile was as sharp and unforgiving as a knife-blade. 'It's an interesting experience,' he said quietly, and leaned over her and opened the door.

Organising the tests didn't take him long. There was a visit to a lawyer, who apparently had to make the arrangements with the testing laboratory. He wanted proofs of identity, so she fossicked around in the small kauri box from beneath Simon's bed that held their important papers and eventually found Simon's birth certificate and her own, and her mother's two marriage certificates.

As she lifted them out an image of a face popped into her mind. Blue, blue eyes and fair powdered hair, a firm chin...

She shook her head, trying to clear it, and the vivid image vanished back into her unconscious as she closed the box and pushed it back beneath the bed.

The solicitor seemed satisfied with the certificates, and, after making notes, told her that Drake himself would collect her the next morning to take them both to the lab.

'You understand that I will be a witness?' he asked.

'Is that necessary?'

'Yes. The legal implications make it imperative. You will sign Drake's blood sample, and he will sign yours, and you'll both sign the child's. I'll sign them all too.'

'I see.' So it was foolproof. Drake wouldn't be able to wriggle out of his responsibility this time. 'I hope you don't mind blood,' she said mischievously.

He gave her a steady, severe look. 'You still have time to back out, Miss Nicholls.'

'No, thank you,' she said crisply.

Fortunately Simon was too excited by the ride in the Jaguar to worry about giving a blood sample. His excitement was compounded by the day off school and the ice-cream that Drake bought him.

Afterwards Drake delivered them back to the flat, gave Olivia that tiger smile, calculating and intimidating, and then said, 'I'll let you know when the results come through. They'll go to the lawyer.'

'How do I know—?' she began, only to fall silent at the warning in his eyes.

'I don't lie,' he said flatly.

She straightened her spine. 'I'll want to see the results,' she warned him.

'Of course.'

He came back just over a week later as Simon was getting into his pyjamas. It had been a fine day, but the evening was crisp and chilly, with the first intimations of winter frosts. Olivia's cold had rallied and returned as bronchitis, and she was sitting in her chair, wretchedly struggling to breathe, when the knock came at the door.

'Who is it?' she asked.

'Drake Arundell.'

Her heart fell into her stomach. Swallowing hard, she got up and let him in.

After one incredulous glance Drake demanded, 'What the hell have you been doing with yourself?'

'Nothing.'

He looked disbelieving, but said crisply, 'The test results have come through.'

'And?' she urged, made uneasy by something in his expression.

At that moment Simon came through the door, waving a small, oval object. 'Is this mine, Liv? I found it in the box under my bed when I was looking for my pencil,' he said, before looking up and breaking into a smile. 'Oh, hello, Mr Arundell.'

Drake looked down at him. No softening appeared in the flinty depths of his eyes, but he said gravely, 'How are you, Simon?'

'Good, thank you.' Hero-worship glowed in Simon's smile. Lately Drake's name had been occurring in his conversation far too often for Olivia's peace of mind. He stuck out his hand and laughed, transferring the little frame to his other hand so that he could shake Drake's outstretched one. 'I found this funny little picture in my box,' he said, 'with the precious papers. Who's the lady, Liv?'

'Let me see that,' Drake said in a quiet, infinitely chilling tone.

Obeying the overt command, Simon obediently handed it over. Drake's long fingers clenched on the delicate image.

Suddenly, her eyes lingering on the face of the woman so skilfully painted, Olivia remembered her dream, and the woman who had told her that she should write to Drake. There she was, very young, her round chin lifted high, large blue eyes solemn and secretive as she looked out at them.

'How odd,' Olivia said involuntarily.

'What is?' Drake's voice was barely audible.

'Oh—I dreamed of her not so long ago.'

In Drake's tanned fingers the dainty lady looked fragile, but there was courage in her sweet face, and more than a hint of wilfulness.

'Where did you get this?' he asked.

Although his voice was calm, almost reflective, and his face completely without expression, the hairs on Olivia's neck lifted. 'It was my mother's,' she said warily. 'She made me promise never to sell it or give it away. I took it with me when I left Springs Flat and kept it in the box, but—it's strange—I forgot completely about it.' She frowned. 'Even when I got our birth certificates out I didn't see it.'

But she had remembered that face...

'Perhaps you dislodged it from wherever it was in the box.' Drake spoke absently, as though that clever mind was somewhere else.

'I must have,' she said, glad that for once her uncertainty wouldn't be as clear to him as the colour of her eyes.

A mysterious tension curled through the silence, thick with unspoken thoughts, hidden meanings. Simon directed an uneasy glance at Olivia.

Smiling at him, she said, 'I'm glad you found the lady, darling. She's lovely, isn't she? I'll have to make sure she doesn't go wandering again. She was very important to Mummy.'

She extended her hand in an imperative movement towards Drake. She could feel his reluctance to relinquish the miniature, but after a moment he put it into her palm, holding it there even as her fingers curled around it until she flicked a startled look upwards. His eyes seared through her, searching, oblique yet piercing, then moved down to the boy between them.

When at last he let the pretty thing go, Olivia had to force herself not to snatch her hand away. She felt as though she had been burned, inside and out, and she sensed in him a bitter, cold fury.

Surely not because he had to face up to his responsibilities?

'So tell me the results,' she said quietly.

His broad shoulders lifted. 'You know what they are,' he said slowly, watching her through half-closed eyes.

Ridiculous to be so consumed by emotion, because she *had* known all along. Unfortunately her quick gasp turned into a bout of coughing; by the time it had run its course she was red-faced, exhaustedly clutching the back of the nearest chair and blinking back the tears that came with each paroxysm.

'Well,' she said hoarsely when she could speak, 'what do we do now?' She took the glass of water Simon had got for her and drank it down, waiting with eagerness for the temporary relief.

Drake's mouth tilted in a flat, humourless smile. 'You'd better start packing.'

'What do you mean?'

He shrugged, his eyes fixed on her white face. She knew she had dark smudges beneath her eyes, and that her skin was sallow and lifeless.

'You're in no fit state to do anything, are you? All right, get your toothbrush and a nightgown. I'll take you both home with me.'

She said feebly, 'I don't—'

'Don't argue.'

She turned, spoiling the dignified effect she hoped to achieve with a sudden lurch that almost precipitated her at his feet. He caught her by the shoulders and lifted her, saying tightly, 'You seem to be making a habit of this.'

Pale, her eyes glittering, she said, 'I am not going to be told what to do—'

'At this moment,' he said caustically, 'you don't look as though you're capable of being anything other than ill. Go on; get just the bare necessities and you can go to bed as soon as we get home.'

It sounded wonderful. She shouldn't, she thought dazedly, agree—but she was going to. Just this once, and then only because she was too tired and too hazy to do anything else...

Olivia never remembered much about the subsequent events of that night, but she did recall Drake's cool assumption of authority, and his expert handling of one sick woman and one extremely excited small boy.

She went to sleep in the car, and was vaguely aware of being carried into a house and upstairs to a warm, dry bedroom. Another spasm of coughing made her gasp for breath as pain shot through her lungs; she barely managed to get into the old T-shirt she wore at night and crawl into bed.

Even then she wasn't allowed to remain peacefully comatose. A strange man came in, poked a thermometer into her mouth, tapped her chest and back, then gave her an injection and several tablets while scolding her for neglecting herself.

At last, drifting into a drug-induced haze, she was able to sleep. It was probably towards morning that a familiar nightmare dragged her gasping and sobbing from the depths of sleep.

'Shh,' a deep male voice said. 'Stop it, Olivia. It's all right.'

The note of exasperation was just what was needed to snap her out of the clutches of the past. She asked huskily, 'Who's that?'

'Drake.' His hand rested on her forehead. 'Your temperature has come down,' he said calmly, as though it was perfectly normal for him to be in her bedroom. 'It must have been some dream. Do you often have nightmares?'

Why had her subconscious decided to produce one that particular night?

'Not often,' she croaked, still dizzy with a combination of drugs and dream. 'Did I wake you up?'

'Yes. You were shrieking like a banshee.'

'What was I yelling?'

'No words, just general screams. They may be infected, but you've got a good pair of lungs.'

Her breath eased out through her lips. 'Simon?' she asked.

'He hasn't stirred.'

'Good,' she said inadequately.

'Is there anything you want?'

'No, thank you.'

He got to his feet and walked noiselessly across the room to a door in the far wall, saying, 'I'll get you a drink.'

She hadn't thought she'd wanted one, but by the time he emerged from what she assumed to be a small bathroom her throat was proclaiming its aridity. 'Thank you,' she said formally.

He watched her while she drank it down, his silent regard making her nervous. When she gave him back the glass he refilled it and left it on the table before saying, 'Don't even think of getting up in the morning. The doctor said you needed rest.'

'All right,' she said meekly. Just until she felt better, she promised herself, she'd let herself be looked after.

'Goodnight, Olivia.'

The door opened; silhouetted against the faint light of a lamp out in the passage he looked large and somehow reassuring, and almost immediately Olivia slid deeply and dreamlessly into oblivion.

She spent most of the next two days sleeping, taking pills and drinking vast amounts of liquids brought up to her by a middle-aged man who told her that his name was Phillips, called her 'miss' and had frown-lines that followed the arches of his brows so that he looked permanently scandalised.

It was Phillips who told her that all of her gear had been packed up and transported from the flat, and that Drake had dealt with the lease and the landlord. Olivia couldn't even rouse herself enough to get angry at this open take-over of her life, or to wonder more than vaguely about Drake's plans. It was, she realised later, a measure of her illness that she was content to drift.

Very much on his best behaviour, Simon spent quite a lot of time in her room. He told her in awe-stricken tones that Drake read stories to him at night, had bought him a Lego set and was listening to him read. And that he was allowed to watch television—'Just one programme, Liv'—every afternoon.

She knew exactly what he'd watched because as soon as the programme had finished he'd race upstairs and act out the whole exciting drama for her.

Each evening Drake came to see how she was. It was an indication of her weakness that she looked forward to those times, even though he never did anything more than survey her keenly and tell her that she looked better and that everything was fine.

After Simon's revelation about the Lego set she thanked Drake. 'It was a lovely thought,' she said a little stiffly.

'Aren't you going to ask me not to spoil him?'

Made uncertain by his sardonic gaze, she pressed her shoulders back into the pillows. 'He could do with some spoiling,' she said shortly. 'But you don't seem to be the sort of man who thinks he can buy love.'

'You might be surprised,' he said, getting gracefully to his feet.

And what, she wondered, watching him from beneath her lashes as he left the room, did he mean by that enigmatic statement? Because if one thing was clear it was that Drake Arundell had never had to buy respect, or love, in his life.

On the morning of the third day she awoke just before dawn and lay beneath the warm covers watching the moon sink behind the curtains. Stretching, she realised that the aches and pains that had belaboured her so unmercifully had gone; she felt fragile, but well. A deep breath reassured her about the state of her lungs. As long as she stayed inside for a few days she'd be fine.

She should be making plans, she thought drowsily. In spite of Drake's actions, common sense told her that he couldn't intend her to live in this house with him. However, she hadn't yet fully recovered from the state of calm, slightly artificial disassociation, where everything seemed ordained and inevitable, so she decided not to worry about the future just yet.

As dawn approached and the sun climbed above the horizon she looked around her room. Walls of the palest yellow gave the room a sunny, fresh ambience, and there were curtains the same colour with a fine blue and grey stripe, the latter colour an exact match for the close-carpeted floor. On the walls hung an eclectic array of pictures—some watercolours of New Zealand landscapes, a large, placid, very muscular bull with a surprisingly small head that had been painted in the eighteenth century, and an exquisite silk embroidery. Her suite was the size of the flat; compared to it, this was heaven.

For the first time since her arrival Olivia was able to appreciate the space and the restrained opulence. After a prodigious yawn she got up and padded across to the bathroom, all marble and mirrors and smooth gleaming surfaces, yet warm in spite of it. Feeling like Cinderella just after a sojourn in the cinders, she peered at herself in the mirror. She looked dreadful—thin and wan, with stark cheekbones and a nose that veered towards the witchlike. The way she looked now, the last thing Drake would want to do was punish her with a kiss!

A curious heat crept stealthily through her veins. Again she wondered—just for a second—what he would be like as a lover. She hadn't ever slept with a man; there simply hadn't been the opportunity. Now she wondered what it would be like to share a bed with Drake, to be at the mercy of his potent masculine strength.

Squelching the unbidden desires by saying jeeringly out loud, 'Don't get hung up on the man. Remember, he left your mother pregnant and carefully avoided finding anything out about his child until you threatened him,' she pulled a hideous grimace at her reflection before showering and washing her hair, then mercilessly scrubbing teeth furred by the night's drugs and lemon drink.

Back in the bedroom, she climbed into a pair of black jeans and a faded peach T-shirt which, along with the rest of her pitifully small wardrobe, Phillips had ironed and put away in the drawers of the long dressing table.

Walking quietly, an odd catch in her throat, she went out and along the passage to the next room.

Still asleep, her brother was huddled beneath the covers, one hand curved around the small black and white toy called Dog after the hero of a popular comic strip. Since he'd begun school Simon wouldn't admit to taking it to bed, but it was always there, his last foothold in infancy. Olivia's eyes filled with sudden tears. She had bought it for him when he was four, paying it off week by week over almost half a year.

As she turned to walk silently out she thought intensely, Whatever happens now, it will be worth it!

Three nights ago she hadn't noticed anything about the house except that it was big and warm and beautifully decorated, with a curving staircase leading upwards from the ground floor.

Now, gazing around, she was impressed. If Drake had chosen the colours and the furniture he had excellent taste. But then, his mother had had great taste. Although Mr Arundell had worked in her stepfather's office, and presumably hadn't earned nearly as much as Brian Harley, their house had been every bit as serene and pleasant as the Harleys'. And that in spite of the very expensive decorator from Auckland whom Elizabeth had hired to refurbish their house.

Olivia had always liked going to the Arundells' home. Drake's mother had been lovely—a quiet woman with a dry sense of humour that had appealed to the young Olivia.

She'd been very ill the year Drake came home for the summer, debilitated by a struggle with cancer. Not that her illness had stopped Brian Harley from sacking her husband when he'd discovered that Drake had fathered his wife's child. The Arundells had moved away from Springs Flat, and only a few months later Olivia had heard of Mr Arundell's death in a road accident. From what Drake had said, his mother was still alive, so she'd won her battle. Olivia hoped that she'd see her again some time.

Following her nose, she walked towards the faint, delectable scent of coffee. Voices from behind a door summoned her; she took a deep breath, stiffened her shoulders, and tilted her chin as she walked in.

At a table in a sunny morning room Drake was reading the newspaper while a radio delivered the morning's dose of misery. A substantial breakfast was spread in front of him. He wore dark trousers and a white shirt—clothes clearly cut to fit his wide shoulders and long arms and legs. The morning sun caught the devil-glow in his hair, turning it to black silk shot with deepest mahogany.

As she came in he stood up, surveying her with a cool, ironic gaze. 'Good morning, Olivia,' he said. 'How are you?'

She couldn't remember ever having seen eyes so totally devoid of expression. One of the reasons for their icy chill was the rim of grey around the edge of the iris, but the elemental lack of emotion had to come from deep within him. What had happened? The Drake she remembered had been confident and compelling, enjoying the charisma of his inborn masculinity, whereas the man looking at her from those remote eyes had worked very hard to build unbreachable defences.

'Good morning,' she said quickly, hiding her instinctive shiver. 'I'm fine, thank you.'

Through another door came Phillips of the permanently astonished look.

'You've met Phillips,' Drake said. 'He's probably the most important person in the house.'

Olivia hid a smile at the reproachful glance the older man gave him. 'Thank you for looking after me so well,' she said, holding out her hand.

Phillips shook it politely but gingerly. 'Good morning, miss. What would you like for breakfast?' he said. 'I'm cooking eggs for Drake; would you like some?'

'An egg would be perfect, thank you, Mr Phillips,' she said.

'Phillips will do, miss,' he said, poker-faced.

She gave him a conspiratorial smile. 'I'll call you Phillips if you'll call me Olivia,' she said cheerfully. 'Otherwise we maintain strict formality.'

He looked as though she'd hit him in the face with an old fish, but she thought she detected the faint glimmer of a smile in his dark eyes.

'Very well, m—Olivia,' he said, and left them alone.

Drake pulled up a chair for her, waited until she'd sat down, then followed suit. 'Phillips will take you to the doctor today for a complete check-up,' he said.

'I'm fine. Really, I am.' It wouldn't be politic to snap that she was, as far as she knew, free of all vermin or diseases, so she confined the flare of defiance to angling her chin at him.

He lifted a saturnine brow. 'You were perilously close to a full collapse.' Nodding at the coffee and orange juice, he continued without any noticeable change in tone, 'What would you like to drink?'

'This looks lovely, thank you.' She poured a glass of orange juice and, noticing that his coffee-cup was empty, asked, 'Do you want more?'

'Thank you.' For some reason her query seemed to amuse him.

Ruffled, she filled his cup before settling back to enjoy the cold, sweet juice.

'So you'll go to the doctor's and you'll do as he says,' he resumed. 'He seemed to think you'd been running on your nerves for too long.'

She said edgily, 'I don't want to be a bother.'

His mouth turned up at the corners. 'Whether you want to be or not, you come under the heading of an attractive nuisance,' he said smoothly. As though his comment had been free from implications, he went on, 'We'd better do something about your driving too. Have you got a licence?'

She flinched. 'Why? What does it matter?' She did have a licence but she was never going to drive again; the accident had shattered what small confidence she'd had in any ability to drive safely.

He got to his feet. 'If you're going to stay here,' he said pleasantly, 'you'll need some sort of transport. Phillips can't run around after you all day; he has other things to do. If you haven't a licence you'll have to get one. If you have, then it sounds as though you need a few tune-up lessons. I'll organise them.'

As a parting shot it couldn't have been bettered. Open-mouthed, Olivia watched him leave the room.

CHAPTER FOUR

SHE was halfway through her breakfast when Simon appeared, his golden eyes wide and a little haunted. 'I wondered where you were,' he said accusingly.

'Good morning, darling.' She gave him a swift, hard hug. 'I'm here, so sit down and have some breakfast.'

Phillips must have had an ear always cocked for the sound of voices. As Simon slid into a chair the older man materialised at the connecting door.

'What would you like for breakfast, Simon?' he asked.

He decided on bacon. 'Seeing,' he explained, 'as Liv is better.' And when Phillips had retired Simon watched with an absorption that held something of awe while Olivia poured him a glass of orange juice.

'I'm glad you're better,' he said. 'This is a nice place, but it's nicer when you're up.'

Touched, she gave him a quick, warm smile. 'Thank you, sir. You'll be able to show me around today. Did you have a good sleep?'

Silly question. Simon always had a good sleep. When he'd emptied the glass and surreptitiously caught a couple of stray drops around his mouth with his tongue, he said seriously, 'Yes. I like sleeping here. Drake's been teaching me how to play draughts. I like it here, Liv,' he reiterated, in case she'd missed the point.

Oh, how easy and peaceful it would be to have a child's unquestioning acceptance! Unfortunately Olivia knew too much about Drake to be comfortable in his house. She definitely didn't want to live here. He was too dangerous and she was too vulnerable. That youthful crush hadn't entirely dissipated during the dark years;

67

he still had the power to make her bones deliquesce, to send a jolt of lightning down her spine.

After she had made their beds and cleaned her bathroom and the battleground that was Simon's, they spent the morning exploring the grounds—some two acres in extent. Simon did the honours with a casual, proprietorial air that worried her, showing her a tennis court and then a swimming pool set behind walls in its own exotic garden, with a pavilion that looked like something out of the Arabian Nights, draped as it was with the last flowers of summer jasmine. Olivia tentatively touched the white waxy blooms, frowning slightly as she inhaled the sweet, exotic perfume.

Clearly it would break Simon's heart if he had to leave these glories. But in spite of Drake's presumption that she'd be living here, he must see that it was impossible. If only she hadn't had bronchitis she could have made it clear to Simon that this was only a visit.

'Drake has a swim here when he comes home from work,' Simon confided. 'He can swim up and down for ages, Liv. He said it's too cold for me.'

She bit her lip. The admiration that coloured his voice wouldn't need much development to become love, and although she had guessed that this might happen, she hadn't accepted it. She wanted to give Simon his chance, but she'd hoped that she would be able to do that without changing their relationship.

She hadn't realised the effect Drake Arundell would have on a child who needed a father.

'Last night some people came to dinner,' Simon said, turning reluctantly away from the pool. 'A lady kissed Drake.'

Olivia looked down at him. His hair, the same honey colour as hers—the same colour as that of their mother— gleamed thick and smooth in the sunlight. He had their golden-brown eyes, their bone structure, fashioned with masculine bluntness. There was nothing of Drake in him at all.

I'm glad, she thought savagely. Perhaps it ran in the family. Drake didn't look like his parents either. He was a throwback to some taller, more compelling ancestor.

'How did you see that happen?' she asked, keeping her tone light. 'Shouldn't you have been in bed?'

He peeped at her from the corner of his eyes. 'I watched from the top of the stairs,' he admitted cheekily. 'But Drake saw me and frowned, so then I went back to bed.'

No discipline problems there.

They were walking slowly across a velvet lawn towards garden beds against a high stone wall bordering a tree-filled gully, probably a reserve. The whole place bore the glossily expensive look of full-time gardening. How on earth had Drake managed to acquire enough money to set himself up like this? Admittedly, he'd earned large amounts on the Formula One circuit before injury had forced his retirement, but surely not enough to buy even the derelict organisation that FuNZ had been, let alone this place?

It must have taken intensely hard work and nerves of steel, as well as a flair for business that bordered on the uncanny. Drake's face sprang into her mind—determined to the point of stubbornness, unyielding and decisive, marked by the signs of a strong will and self-reliance. Her mouth curved into an almost wistful smile.

If anyone could do it, she thought, Drake could.

Apart from the pool, the place Simon liked most was the orchard, where tropical-looking tamarillo trees and feijoas and mandarins joined with late apples in a symphony of ruby and green and vivid orange. They ate a tamarillo each, relishing its tangy, sub-acid flesh.

Made pleasantly drowsy by the sun, Olivia watched Simon pick up several of the largest feijoas and went with him when he carried them triumphantly into the kitchen.

Phillips accepted them, agreed—after a quick, questioning look at Olivia—that one wouldn't spoil Simon's lunch, and while the boy was demolishing the sweet, jelly-like flesh with its intriguing flavour of musk and pineapple, told Olivia that her appointment with the doctor was at two o'clock. Simon was to go as well.

Mentally reviewing her brother's wardrobe, Olivia thanked him, and they went outside to resume their exploration. This time Simon showed her a pretty deck with a view of the sea beneath a massive old pohutukawa sporting branches that were perfect for climbing. As he demonstrated.

'Do you like it?' he asked from his perch three feet above the ground. 'It's just like a park, isn't it?' That possessive note was back in his voice.

'Indeed it is.' It had to be impossible in such a short time, but his eyes sparkled, his skin had a healthy flush, and it almost seemed as though he'd put on weight. He certainly looked happier.

Suspending himself beneath a branch, he waited for her to admire his cleverness, then asked with an elaborately casual air, 'Are we going to live here?'

Crunch time. She said carefully, 'I don't know, darling. I have to talk to Drake.'

'I want to live here. I like it,' he said in an aggressive tone, then jumped down and walked away, his back stiff and resentful.

Olivia looked over the wide lawn, at borders bright with the last of the autumn roses, and thought worriedly that this conversation should have come after she had talked to Drake. Simon had stopped and was kicking at the grass, casting little looks at her to see her reaction. 'It would mean going to a different school,' she warned him.

He turned his head, more intrigued than intimidated. 'I wouldn't mind,' he said scornfully. 'Don't you want to live here?'

'It's lovely, isn't it?' She couldn't give him a direct answer. All she knew was that she had no intention of giving Simon up. 'But Drake might not want us to live here, darling. This isn't our home.'

'I want it to be,' Simon shouted, and ran back up to the house, ignoring her calls to stop.

You, she thought, apostrophising the woman in the miniature, have a lot to answer for! Look what happens when I let myself be influenced by you.

Nothing had worked out the way she'd anticipated. Drake had walked into her life and overturned it with such cool mastery that she was left stumbling.

At one-thirty, with Simon over his paddy and dressed in his best shorts and shirt, and Olivia in a straight skirt of a somewhat muddy shade of green and a short-sleeved blouse in white with a bow at the neck, Phillips drove them to the surgery in a small Japanese car that bore a distinct resemblance to a Jeep.

They were given a thorough examination. The doctor—the same man who had come to the house when Olivia and Simon had arrived that night—took especial care to check her lungs and throat before going over Simon with equal exhaustiveness.

'I'll make an appointment to have the grommets put in,' he said, when it was all over and Simon was playing quietly in a corner with a wonderful truck set. 'It will mean a full day at a clinic.'

Olivia nodded.

'You're in reasonable shape, although I want you to watch your diet and your activity for the next couple of months. You came close to a complete collapse, as I'm sure you realise.'

'Drake told me,' she said tonelessly.

The doctor looked at her with wry amusement. 'I'll bet he did. He was very worried, and rightly so. To put it bluntly, you were a mess. Never let a bout of bronchitis go so far again. That's what doctors are for, you know.'

If you've got the money to pay them, she thought, smiling, nodding.

'Ah, well,' the doctor said comfortably, looking down at Simon, who, oblivious to everything, was absorbed in the delights of heavy construction, 'I've no doubt the redoubtable Phillips will keep you on the straight and narrow now.'

Nobody asked for payment, so Olivia assumed that Drake was paying for her as well as Simon. When she was able she'd make sure that every cent he'd spent on her was repaid.

His insinuation that she saw him as a money tree hurt. But she wasn't going to think about that now. She'd had enough of being swept up like a bit of flotsam—or was it jetsam?—and carried along on the force of Drake's will.

They needed to talk, she decided as she and Simon walked out into the warm sunlight, and the first thing she wanted to discuss was how to make sure that Simon was safe, with the threat that her stepfather represented well and truly blocked. There must be some way to get over the fact that Simon was registered as his son.

'There's Drake!' Simon announced delightedly, running ahead towards the car park. To her astonishment Drake was getting out of the green Jaguar, the red lights in his hair gleaming in the brisk sunlight. He didn't ask how they had got on, although his glance at Olivia was keen and too perceptive.

Instead of going home, he took them to the Museum of Transport and Technology. Olivia would have preferred to return to Judge's Bay; the noise and traffic had conspired to give her a headache. However, Simon was so incandescently happy about this unexpected treat that she'd have crawled over broken glass rather than spoil it.

It was a small foretaste of purgatory. People stared, and the skirt and blouse she had thought reasonably fashionable when she'd put them on were displayed in all their dowdiness. What made it worse was that Drake's compelling male magnetism was intensified rather than muted by a suit cut by an expert. Not, she suspected, made in New Zealand either; this looked like English styling. Beside him she was drab and far too conspicuous.

Her embarrassment wasn't helped by the way other women looked at him from beneath their lashes, or with swift, sideways glances. Olivia they dismissed with something like amused horror, but when their eyes came to rest on Drake they were more than appreciative— some, she noted, were distinctly predatory. To Olivia's shock she discovered in herself a mean, proprietorial inclination.

Dog in the manger, she warned sternly. You don't want him; you just don't want anyone else to want him.

It would be dangerous to get any more entangled with Drake Arundell than she already was. If it weren't for Simon she'd be pleased never to see him again.

And, firmly repressing a traitorous suspicion that she was being a little less than honest with herself, she trailed along with them, pretending to enjoy the occasion as much as her brother so clearly was.

Somehow Simon discovered that Drake had once driven a racing car, and from then on spent most of the time plying him with questions, soaking up the answers with a wide-eyed fascination that increased her uneasiness. Until that afternoon Simon had been in love with dinosaurs, but she could see that his new knowledge of Drake's exploits had completely vanquished their hold on his imagination.

'Did you have some accidents?' Simon asked, that incipient hero-worship glinting in his eyes.

Drake answered him with the grave courtesy of one adult to another. 'Yes.'

Simon's eyes rounded. 'Did you get hurt?'

'Not too badly.'

Well, no, of course he hadn't, Olivia thought tartly. He was far too confident, far too competent to damage himself severely. Nothing ever went wrong for Drake Arundell. He was proper hero material.

She said, 'That last accident must have been pretty serious.'

It had put an end to his career. She remembered how upset she had been, and how surprised that her mother hadn't seemed overly worried. But by that time Elizabeth had had more immediate concerns than the health of her ex-lover, she thought acidly. Keeping sane and alive, for example.

'I was lucky,' he said. 'It did me very little harm beyond slowing my reflexes.'

'But that's why you gave it up?'

'One of the reasons.' He looked down at her with hooded eyes and an enigmatic smile. 'Fast reflexes are vitally important in the motor racing world, but the reason I gave up was that when I began racing I locked myself into a contract with a manager to invest my earnings from the sport, and I discovered that he was systematically cheating me. The only way to break his hold over my income was to give up racing.'

Horrified, Olivia stared at him. 'How did you get into such a predicament?'

His mouth twisted. 'I was young and stupid and grateful. It was a hard lesson, but it taught me never to trust anyone—not even a benefactor.'

For some reason his words chilled her; it was an indication of his rigorous determination that rather than allow himself to be cheated he'd given up his chance at fame as well as the career he'd fought for.

Grateful for Simon's request to be told the most exciting thing that ever happened to him, she listened while Drake described an incident involving another car that had crashed into a tractor and exploded on a country road miles from anywhere. He made it sound remarkably prosaic, but it was obvious that he'd acted with cold, intelligent courage.

'Ooh,' Simon breathed, agog with admiration. 'I'd be scared.'

'I was terrified,' Drake told him calmly. 'So was everyone else, but fear is no excuse for not doing things.'

Frowning, Olivia looked from her brother's entranced face to that of the man with them. Drake was watching her, sardonic amusement crystallising in his eyes. Colour drained from her skin as she stared back at him. One dark, winged brow lifted in a taunting question, and hastily Olivia looked away. For the rest of the trip around the museum she said little; it was almost difficult to smile whenever Simon looked at her. Which wasn't often.

It was hard to accept that she was petty enough to resent her brother's absorption in Drake. She felt small and cheap, but she couldn't rid herself of the snaky tendrils of jealousy that threatened to ruin her composure—and her image of herself.

Back at Judge's Bay, Olivia waited until Simon had raced into the kitchen to tell Phillips where they had been and what he'd seen, then said without preamble, 'We need to talk.'

'Certainly. Will tomorrow be soon enough? I'm afraid I have to go out this evening.'

'Yes, of course,' she said distantly.

She and Simon ate dinner in the breakfast room before settling down to explore the ramifications of the stereo and CD set-up hidden behind doors in the wall—Simon amazing her by showing her how the extremely complicated and upmarket equipment worked. Drake had told him, he informed her nonchalantly.

Relaxing into the comfortable sofa, Olivia let the music flow through her while on the floor at her feet Simon drew on a sheet of white paper with a huge new box of coloured pens. Racing cars, she noticed, not dinosaurs.

'Drake bought these pens for me,' he said proudly when he noticed her interest. 'Aren't they great, Liv?'

'Very handsome.'

It had been years since she had listened to music; she hadn't realised just how much she missed it. Light opera had been a favourite of Elizabeth's, and as the well-remembered tunes floated through the room tears pricked the back of Olivia's eyes.

How could Drake have made love to her mother, impregnated her, and then just left her?

Sixteen years older than he was, Elizabeth Harley had been trapped in an unhappy marriage. Olivia had always known that her mother and her stepfather didn't have much in common, but with the self-absorption of the young she had simply accepted the situation, finding it easier because they had never quarrelled in front of her.

And probably because she didn't remember Elizabeth's first marriage, which had apparently been idyllic. Olivia's father had died in a boating accident three months before she was born.

Perhaps if the Harleys had had children it might have helped, but for some reason there had been none. Looked at with adult eyes, Elizabeth's behaviour was simple enough to understand—a desperate attempt to regain her lost youth, to prove that she was still desirable, possibly a last, reckless reaching towards the love she'd feared was forever beyond her reach. Had she agonised over the subtle evidences of fading beauty, needing the reassurance of Drake's uncomplicated lust?

But how could he have flirted with the daughter while making love to the mother? Perhaps he'd been unable to restrain himself, Olivia thought cynically, or perhaps he was simply a predator, taking whatever he wanted.

That possibility sent a furious, sick shudder through Olivia, an angry stab of betrayal. With the music her mother had loved filling the serene room, she told herself as she had so many times that the past wasn't important, except that Simon, too young and innocent to be able to defend himself, needed help, and unfortunately at the moment the only person able to give it was the man who had abandoned him before his birth.

She let him stay up a little later than normal. He wanted to watch television but she shook her head, saying, 'No, not tonight. It says in the paper that there's a really good programme on tomorrow, so we'll wait until then.'

Although the presence of television in his new life fascinated him, Simon gave in with comparatively good grace. The tantrums that had become a regular part of their life seemed to be in abeyance; rewarding his forbearance, she spent an extra ten minutes reading to him, and paid for it with a strained throat.

It was getting harder to sustain the effort needed now; his hearing was deteriorating fast. The doctor had said that he should have grommets in place within the week and she could hardly wait. If his teacher was right, the tantrums should disappear as soon as he could hear properly.

After kissing him goodnight she went back to her room, wondering rather forlornly what she should do with the rest of the evening. Exhaustion weighted her limbs, and, as well as her throat, the headache that had been threatening since the afternoon seemed intent on making a nuisance of itself.

A slow survey of her tasteful, impersonal room persuaded her that she wanted nothing more than to have a long bath and read in bed until she dropped off to sleep. She walked down the staircase to the morning room and collected several magazines from a rack. She was interrupted by Phillips, whom she asked if he had an aspirin.

'There should be some in your bedroom,' he said, looking at her keenly.

'I didn't look there.' She smiled. 'Goodnight.'

'Goodnight, m—Olivia.'

Magazines in hand, she wandered back to her room. At the flat she'd revelled in her time to read with an intensity that came from its very rarity. Now, with as much time as she wanted ahead of her, she couldn't settle.

After a long, warm wallow in water made fragrant and silky by a few drops of sweet-scented oil, she took an aspirin from the packet she'd found in the cupboard and went to bed. Half an hour's dogged pleasure in the magazines was enough; besides, the aspirin had made her feel floaty and light-headed.

Leaning back against the pillows, she gazed at her hands. Although she'd been using the sinfully rich hand lotion she'd found in a bathroom cupboard along with other toiletries, it hadn't yet had a chance to make much difference. Against the fine white percale sheets they looked rough and uncared-for.

Like the rest of her, she thought, running her fingers through her hair. It was almost six months since she'd been able to afford to have it cut, and even then it had been the amateurish attempt of a girl from one of the other flats. She didn't need a mirror to tell her that it was long and untidy and unkempt.

And her old, worn T-shirt must be the strangest night attire ever worn in this bed. Like the haircut, it hadn't been expensive to start off with, and the slogan on the front was long washed off, leaving only a faint, shadowed pattern above her breasts.

Amazingly, she was lying in this huge bed, protected and safe for the first time in years, not needing to worry about the power bill, and instead of enjoying it she was pining for the cramped, noisy, shabby flat! Her eyes flicked across to the wardrobe. It gave her a warm feeling to know that safely ensconced at the bottom of it was her old sewing machine.

Part of the problem, she decided, trying to look at it objectively, was the loss of control. The last five years hadn't been easy or pleasant, but at least she'd been in charge. Well, as much in charge as she could be when she was constrained by Simon's needs.

Now she was in an entirely equivocal position. She had tacitly relinquished her claim on Simon, and had no claim on Drake at all. If he wanted to, he could simply toss her out and she'd have to go.

A tap on her door made her turn her head. Hastily she pulled the sheet up past her breasts and called out, 'Come in.'

It wasn't Phillips, as she'd half-expected, checking to make sure she was all right. Instead Drake stood in the doorway.

Formally he asked, 'May I come in?'

'Well, yes, I suppose so.' She licked her lips and wondered whether she should have said no, but he was already inside—although, she noted, he didn't close the door behind him.

He'd taken off his dinner jacket and slung it over his shoulder, so the white shirt gleamed softly in the subdued light of the bedside lamp. Olivia's heart blocked her throat as he strode across the room, dropped the jacket in the armchair and came to a halt beside the bed. She felt suffocated and yet unbearably alive, little flames of awareness flickering in a wildfire pattern through her.

He said, 'You're looking a bit wan. How's the headache?'

'Who told you?' she asked, and then, remembering, said, 'Oh, Phillips, I suppose?'

'Yes. How is it?'

'It's all right,' she said quickly. 'Thank you.' Had he come here to ask about her head?

'So,' he said, 'what do you want to talk to me about, Olivia?'

Fixing her eyes on the floor, she said, 'I need to know what's happening.'

'Why?'

'Because I need to know,' she said stubbornly. 'Simon shouldn't be away from school for too long.'

'He looks as though he could do with a decent rest,' Drake said without expression.

'He's already behind in his school work.' She looked up sharply, met cool speculation in his eyes and had to fight to keep her gaze steady.

'Once he's had his ears done he'll catch up. He's a bright kid.'

She sent him a glittering glance. 'I know. But—I'd like to know what plans you've made.' She took a deep breath. 'I can't just stay here...'

'If you want to live with Simon that's just what you'll have to do.'

Not a hint of kindness or understanding softened his features or his words; it was, she realised, an ultimatum.

She looked uncertainly at him, resenting the command he had over his emotions. 'You don't want me here,' she said, knowing as she spoke that for her this was the unwelcome crux of the matter.

'You were the one who said I should take responsibility for Simon. You were, of course, quite right.' Mockery tinged his deep voice, smoothing for a second the sensual roughness. 'It's a pity you don't want to live here, but you can't have everything your own way, Olivia. Life is a series of compromises, after all.'

'I know that,' she snapped.

He lifted his brows and said thoughtfully, 'Yes, you do, don't you. That was unfair of me.'

She hated it when he looked at her like that, as though she was something small and ineffectual, a person to be pitied. 'It's going to be an awful nuisance for you—'

'Oh, the house is big enough to take us all. Don't worry about it.'

She almost ground her teeth. 'I don't want to end up so far in your debt that I'll never be able to repay you.'

He said curtly, 'You can forget about trying to repay me. With the two thousand you owe your neighbour and your board and lodging you'll be in my debt for ever.'

Swift cat's-paws of shock shivered across her determined composure. Something prowled behind the blunt words—something that was not to her advantage. 'I don't want you to pay Brett,' she said, appalled. 'That's not why I contacted you.'

Beneath the half-closed lids his eyes gleamed cat-like—silver-green and unblinking. 'Really? How foolish of me—I thought it was one of the reasons you contacted me. It's too late to tell me that now—I've already paid him off.'

'I'll pay you back!'

'How? By sewing?' He eyed the swift colour bolting through her skin with cynical amusement. 'If you're so determined to repay me you can become my mistress.'

She stared at him as though he had gone mad. Instinct warned her that to give in to outraged fury would put her at a complete disadvantage. She said huskily, 'You've got a nerve. I suppose if I say go to hell you'll throw me out?'

'If I answered yes to that, would you agree?'

'No!'

'And I'm not quite so much of a swine as to throw you out.'

She couldn't think clearly, and when she moved her bones felt weighted, lax. The cool, heavy fall of her hair swung against her neck, scented by shampoo he had paid for—as he had also paid for the soap and oil whose perfume was a delicate whisper across her skin.

In a low, shamed voice she said, 'I'm going to forget you ever said that.' Her pulses were running wild, driving a fiery excitement through her. For a moment—a heated moment—she'd been tempted.

'Will you be able to?' His gaze burned through the flimsy veil of her composure. 'You're good at running away, aren't you? But you can't run away from that, Olivia. I want you, and you want me too.'

'I do not!'

His mouth twisted into a smile. 'Lie to yourself if you must. However, don't expect me to go along with your misconceptions,' he said, unruffled, the green dying from his eyes to leave them as cold and pitiless as the distant stars.

'Just because I was taken by surprise when you kissed me once—'

'Come on, Olivia, you can do better than that.' Impatient sarcasm told her what he thought of her feeble excuse. 'Do you think I'm so inexperienced I don't know when a woman is attracted to me?'

'I think you're an arrogant, conceited swine,' she blazed.

'And you're a coward. Are you taken by surprise now? Let's see, shall we?' he said almost casually, and sat down on the side of the bed and bent his head.

Olivia put up her hand, but he caught it in his, effortlessly holding her still. Betrayed by her own body, she forgot everything she had learned about defending herself. The kiss was at once a naked exercise of power and intense seduction, and to her horror and humiliation Olivia had no resistance—not even when one of his hands cupped her breast, the long fingers stroking with insistent authority through the soft, worn material of her shirt.

Dazed, almost bewildered by the white-hot ve-
hemence of the sensations roaring through her with the
force of a runaway train, Olivia lifted weighted eyelids
and said indistinctly, 'No—not this...'

'You are beautiful,' he said against her mouth, and
something, some odd note almost like anger in his voice,
stopped the words that stumbled to her lips. 'Hair the
colour of dark honey, and golden eyes that hide secrets,
and skin so warm and rich I want to touch you all the
time...'

The sensuous texture of his voice flowed smoothly over
her quaking nerves, seducing her with sound alone. If
he had tried to do anything more she would have resisted, for in spite of the violent responses of her body
she was afraid—afraid that he had a hidden agenda, that
it wasn't desire that was driving him.

The hand shaping her breast stilled. His mouth barely
touched hers, yet she couldn't move, couldn't free her
mouth from the wild sorcery of that light pressure. Her
mind told her to pull back while there was still time, but
the roiling storm of need his touch and closeness had
engendered proved the stronger, seething through her
thwarted body, insistent, expectant, clamorous.

'Damn you, Drake,' she muttered.

'What do you want?'

She managed to jerk her head back so that she could
meet his eyes. It was the worst mistake she could have
made because immediately she was lost, chained with
shackles of emerald fire.

Yet still he didn't move.

Summoning all of her willpower, Olivia dragged her
gaze away from the mesmerising imprisonment of his.
Willy-nilly her eyes fell to the sculptured curves of his
mouth, a little fuller than normal with the pressure of
that seeking, demanding kiss.

Sensation, keen and inexorable as the blade of a sword, shot down her spine, gathered in a tight knot deep in the pit of her stomach, began to churn and heat.

'You are beautiful'...

His words echoed in her mind. Olivia wondered sickly whether Elizabeth had been ensnared by these fetters of desire, this savage need, darker, infinitely more powerful than the imperatives which had driven her mother before then. Had just such a hungry languor as this led to Simon's conception?

'No!' she said stormily, pain and a bitter anger lending her unnatural strength as she jerked back from the hand that lay so confidently against her breast, her expression revealing the profundity of her sudden, intense revulsion.

His eyes narrowed, scanned her face, lingered on the throbbing heat of her mouth. 'Why not?' he asked unhurriedly.

With fierce resentment she said, 'Will it give you some perverted enjoyment to make comparisons between my mother and me?'

A muscle flicked against the slashing line of his jaw. Sculpted eyelids hid everything but a thin sliver of pure, saturated green. In a swift, graceful movement he got to his feet, saying curtly, 'I don't make comparisons. Ever. And however you try to deny it, Olivia, there's something unfinished between us. When you're ready, we'll see where it takes us.'

Despair ached through her. 'I'll never be ready,' she snapped. 'I despise you.'

'I can see that.' His mouth twisted. With cruel deliberation he said, 'I find it exciting. The calm exterior, and beneath it that rare, blazing passion.'

Her lashes flew up. She could find no sign of emotion in his face, nothing but a hard-edged mockery that humiliated her. 'I don't even like you,' she said, trying to fight him with the only weapons she had—words.

He gave a short, mirthless laugh. 'Liking has nothing to do with it. That was a straight exchange of need—a chemical reaction, if you like. You can't deny it, however inconvenient it might be.'

'Just like that—so cold-blooded.'

'There was nothing cold-blooded about that kiss,' he said brutally.

She sought something to frighten him off. 'I'd be stupid to let you get me pregnant like you did my mother,' she said, emphasising her words with pointed cruelty.

His face went rigid, but he spoke without heat. 'That won't happen.'

The prospect, however remote, of being pregnant with his child filled her with a bewildered complexity of emotions, the most obvious of which was horror. She said angrily, 'No, it's impossible.'

'Why?' He looked down, studying the slender lines of her body beneath the covers.

If she explained that the thought of him in bed with her mother made her feel sick, might he not suspect that her heart was involved as well as her body?

Indeed, she was beginning to wonder whether the emotion that spiked through her whenever she thought of that liaison was jealousy.

She looked at him, at the strong, blunt contours of his face, the lean, long torso, heavily muscled and powerful. No sign of gentleness, of tenderness, in any part of him; nothing but raw, feral potency.

She said, 'I'm not capable of being purely pragmatic about such things—' She stopped, heat sweeping in a blush of peach across her skin. Rallying, she continued, 'And this is coming close to sexual harassment!'

'Very well, then,' he said. 'Leave it.'

She said defensively, 'I want to pay my way, Drake, but—not like that.'

'All right, you've made your feelings clear,' he said absently.

With gritty determination she plunged on, 'It's just that I've never actually thought of myself as a whore before.'

He fixed her with an aloof, unimpressed gaze. 'Grow up, Olivia. What do you want me to say?' he asked, each soft word clear and precise. 'That I don't consider you a whore?'

Confused, because of course that was exactly what she wanted from him, even though his actions belied such a statement, she returned vigorously, 'Well, I'm not.'

'I have no intention of treating you as one,' he said, apparently bored by the whole embarrassing discussion. 'What we'd have would be a mutually satisfactory arrangement. However, as I said before, that is not important. Do you want to know my plans for Simon's future?'

'You know perfectly well I do!'

'Very well, then He stays here. That is not negotiable.' A relentless note in his voice warned her that he meant it.

CHAPTER FIVE

OLIVIA'S troubled gaze met a stone wall—immovable, uncompromising. 'What about me?' she asked in a subdued voice.

'You wanted to go to university,' he said, watching her.

'Yes,' she returned, trying to conceal just how painful her abandoned ambitions were. 'I'm surprised you remember.'

She shouldn't have said that. The words revealed just how much she recalled of that long-ago summer when she'd thought he was seeing her as an adult instead of the schoolgirl she'd been—the summer when he'd used her open adoration, her childish crush, to conceal his affair with Elizabeth.

'I remember. If you stay here as Simon's "mother" I'll pay your university fees.'

She cast him a glance in which longing was compounded with a bleak savagery and snapped, 'And in return you'd expect me to sleep with you. I won't be pressured—'

'No.' He sounded matter-of-fact, as though dealing with a purely business matter. For him it obviously was. 'I've never had to buy sex and I'm not starting now. The last thing I want in my bed is a woman who grits her teeth and thinks of her bank balance when I make love to her. That's what being a whore is all about—not honest passion honestly expressed.' His tone was made complex by double-edged mockery. 'You were cheated of a life when you decided to make yourself responsible for Simon. I'm offering you another chance.'

'But there are conditions.'

His smile was as cynical as her tone. 'There are always conditions. You stay here with Simon. And you never, under any circumstances, mention his parentage to anyone.'

Her swift, unthinking reply was forestalled by a lean, uplifted hand.

'That's not negotiable either. As for living here, once you decide to stop being coy you'll see that it will have advantages for all of us. Simon, for example, will keep the only mother he can remember.'

She looked up quickly. 'Did you ask him about—?'

'Elizabeth? Yes.' His eyes were shadowed, unreadable, but she mistrusted the sardonic twist of his mouth. 'You've done an excellent job of sanctifying her for him. I didn't recognise her when he talked about her. However, she's just a nebulous, angelic figure in the back of his mind, rather as your own father must be to you.

'For all practical purposes you are Simon's mother. And he needs stability. In return for being here with him and putting off marriage—because you're going to sign a contract saying that you won't leave him until he's reached secondary school age—you get more salubrious surroundings, an allowance and a future.'

Narrowed eyes noted her ambivalence, because he finished blandly, 'I travel a lot, so I won't be able to look after him. Phillips has enough to do without acting as nursemaid, even if he wanted to—which he doesn't. And of course you will both get whatever protection I organise against your father.'

'And what do you get?'

'A son. And repayment of your debt to me. It's the only way you'll be able to do it. I don't need money. I already have a housekeeper and a gardener and someone to mend my clothes. I don't even need a hostess, or a wife. But I do need a mother for Simon.'

She bit her lip. If she was truthful it was exactly what she wanted, but it seemed too easy... Olivia had learned that there was always a price to pay.

As well, there was that kiss.

'And no—harassment?' she blurted, fixing him with a glittering golden glare.

His mouth twitched. 'No harassment,' he said solemnly.

'All right, then,' she said.

He extended his hand. After a torn moment she put hers into it. Almost immediately he lifted hers and searched the calluses out with a steady finger, a frown drawing his brows together.

'What caused these?' he asked brusquely, looking up suddenly as he let her reclaim her hand.

She shrugged. 'Using scissors a lot.'

'Did you work in a factory?'

'No, I was an outworker.'

'For how long?'

Her fingers pulled at the sheet, folding and crimping it. 'Three years. From when Simon and I came to Auckland until a few days before I wrote to you.'

'How did the spoilt, pampered child I remember learn to work so hard?'

'It's a skill like any other. I had good teachers,' she retorted shortly, thinking of all the people who had helped her without thought of reward or repayment, from Emma and Neil to the house truck gypsies who had welcomed her into their loose, friendly society.

'Why didn't you get help from Child Welfare?'

'And get my name on a computer list? They'd only have had to check to realise Simon wasn't mine, and then they'd have taken him away from me.'

He said abruptly, 'They wouldn't have been likely to return a child to a father who'd abused him.'

'You're his father, damn you!' She reined in a sudden hot tumble of words, adding in a slightly more conciliatory tone, 'I'm sure the welfare people would have done their best, but they're too short-staffed to do much more than keep their heads above water. Logically, my stepfather looks much more likely to give Simon a better life than the sister who ran away with him and spent the next two years picking apples! The only way to keep Simon safe is for you to accept responsibility for him.'

He had walked across to the chair and picked up his dinner jacket, but at her words he swung around. 'I've already done that,' he said curtly, looking down at the dark material in his hands. Light tangled in the lashes shadowing his eyes, so that she couldn't read his emotions. 'What makes you think your stepfather wants Simon? From what I remember of him he's not likely to enjoy watching the fruit of his wife's affair grow up bearing his name.'

Olivia threw him an aggressive glance. 'He registered Simon as his.'

'I know. What I don't know is why.'

'To punish Mother. By doing that he had power over her and Simon. He liked power.'

'You're describing a man who's scarcely sane,' he said dispassionately, as though the subject was of purely academic interest.

She shivered. 'I don't think he is.'

'Perhaps he just wants a son. Did he have any contact with his daughter from his first marriage?'

'No.' As far as Olivia knew neither Brian's child nor his ex-wife had ever communicated with him. Their names certainly hadn't ever been mentioned in the house at Springs Flat. 'If he does want a son it will still be a power thing. I tell you, he hates Simon.'

He didn't look as though he disbelieved her, but she could tell from his remote expression that he wasn't entirely convinced. Eager to leave the distasteful subject of her stepfather, Olivia asked tentatively, 'Drake, from the way you spoke of her, I assume your mother's still alive?'

After a slight hesitation, he said, 'Yes, she is.'

'I'm so glad,' she said, smiling. 'I wondered, because she was awfully sick that last year at Springs Flat. It's wonderful that she recovered. Where is she now?'

'In Canada.' He slung the jacket over his shoulder. As he turned to go he said, 'Tomorrow Phillips will take you shopping. You and Simon both need complete new wardrobes.'

At the automatic shake of her head he said inflexibly, 'I'm having a dinner party on Saturday night.'

'I won't—'

'Don't be an idiot. You'll be there!' His features hardened into a mask that was all forceful command. 'I'm not having you cower away in your bedroom like a poor relation. You can come out of that self-imposed exile—'

'No,' she broke in. 'If I start going out, sooner or later someone will tell my stepfather! You know how small New Zealand is—you can't keep a secret however much you try!'

'To hell with your stepfather!' His voice was cold and deliberate.

When she opened her mouth to protest he cut her off with quiet ruthlessness. 'If you don't show me a respectably festive dress tomorrow night I'll take you into Auckland and buy you something myself, and if necessary I'll stand over you while you put it on on Saturday night!'

He meant it. She said frigidly, 'There's no need to go to those extremes. All right, I'll buy myself something that won't make everyone wonder whether I've just emerged from under a dustbin lid. And I'll wear it to your dinner party. Now, I'm tired; do you mind going?'

'Not in the least,' he returned, walking towards the door. 'Get a decent haircut while you're about it. Goodnight, Olivia. Sleep well.'

She would also keep score, she vowed as the door closed behind him, so that if—no, *when*—she achieved her ambitions she'd be able to pay back every cent he'd spent on her.

As she lay there in the darkness, safe and comfortable in the luxury of his home, she knew that she was going to accept his offer to pay her university fees. With a degree under her belt she could find a job and begin to pay him back.

There was another reason too. If she didn't fill her life with something exhilarating and time-consuming, something that kept her mind busy, sooner or later she'd give in to the compelling magnetic pull he had for her.

The prospect made her feel sick. It was humiliating enough to want the man who had seduced and abandoned her mother, but to surrender to it and make love with him, knowing that he would be merely using her to appease a physical need—oh, that would be utterly crushing.

Once more she shivered at the clutch of primal warmth in her loins, the shaming desire that warned her how close she was to yielding.

If she let it happen she'd hate herself until the day she died. Unfortunately, for Simon's sake, she had to stay here. No mother who'd carried him under her heart for nine months could love him more, and she wanted him to be happy, to be secure. Tearing his life apart for her own selfish reasons wouldn't add to his happiness or his well-being.

So she'd go to university and work hard until eventually this bitter need would die of starvation and she'd be able to look at Drake with nothing more than mild affection.

So accustomed was she to the glare of the streetlight through thin curtains that this darkness seemed almost smothering. She closed her lashes and guiltily let herself recall the kiss.

Just this once, she promised her sensible self.

Something about Drake's open sexuality had changed the way she thought about herself. When his mouth had touched hers she'd lost the level head she'd developed over the years and reverted right back to the star-struck seventeen-year-old she had been when he'd first kissed her.

The reason was obvious; while other women her age had been gaining experience and a healthy dose of cynicism she'd been locked away as safely as Sleeping Beauty, using Simon as her fence of thorns, afraid that if she allowed anyone to get close it might somehow lead to discovery and Simon's return to a man who hated him.

So she had nothing to base any comparison on. That was why she still wanted Drake; he had been the first and last man she had fallen in love with, and she had never grown beyond him.

Not that it meant anything to him; she might be almost totally innocent, but she knew damned well that the kiss had started out as a punishment.

For making life difficult for him by popping up again like a demon in a pantomime, forcing him to face and accept his responsibilities?

It had to be that.

Shaken by a gust of furious anger, she lay mulling it over until eventually she slid into a restless and troubled sleep.

She woke the next morning fired by a militancy that stayed through her shower. When muffled sounds through the wall indicated that Simon had stirred, she went in to find him dressing in the secondhand jeans she had picked up for a song at a street market.

Misinterpreting her mood, he said defiantly, 'I want to wear these.'

'Nobody's stopping you,' she said, sneaking a hug. He still gave her a goodnight kiss without any objections, but his attitude to cuddles had changed since he'd started school. It was natural, but she missed his open, candid affection. This time, however, he returned the hug.

It tempered her aggression, but it was with high colour and glittering golden eyes that she went down the stairs.

Drake got to his feet and smiled at them both. He had a wicked smile, dazzling and sexy as hell, reinforced by eyes hooded into lazy sensuality.

'Good morning,' he said.

'Good morning,' they chorused.

He put Olivia into her chair and sat down as Phillips appeared. During the next few minutes Olivia had to impress upon Simon that bacon was not to be his regular breakfast. The short tussle of wills was won by Olivia, although Simon didn't settle down to muesli, fruit and milk until after a quiet command from Drake.

Before Drake left for work he drew her to one side and said, 'By the way, your stepfather is now permanently based in Australia. If he does hear about your re-emergence it certainly won't be until after my lawyer and I have worked out how to deal with the situation.'

She shivered, but said nothing, and after a moment he resumed, 'I'm looking forward to seeing your dress for Saturday night. And the new hair. I'll get Maria to make an appointment for you at Mirelle.'

'They'll probably be booked out,' she snapped.

His brows lifted. 'Not for me,' he said softly.

She bared her teeth at him and he laughed, flicked her cheek with a casual finger, and said goodbye to Simon.

* * *

The shopping expedition taxed her strength, mainly because Phillips displayed a mulish persistence that exhausted her into buying more for Simon than she otherwise would have done.

'Right, that's it,' she said after she had chosen Simon's outfits.

'I'm sorry, m—Olivia?' Phillips sounded surprised.

Simon was gazing with awe at the pile of clothes they had accumulated. Never in his remembrance had he had two sets of brand new trousers and shirts, as well as a pair of shoes and two pairs of socks.

'That's all he needs,' Olivia said firmly.

Phillips looked obstinate. 'I checked with a young lady down the road last night. She has a boy the same age as Simon, and she gave me a list of clothes he'd need.' To Olivia's astonishment he removed a sheet of paper from his wallet, opened it and read it aloud. 'Quite a lot more,' he observed mildly in the short silence that followed.

Olivia knew when she was beaten, but she felt guilty and uneasy, as though by letting Drake pay she had somehow ceded much more than she should have. However, the delight in her brother's face when he realised that, as well as the hard-wearing sensible clothes she had already chosen, he was to have a brightly coloured anorak and a pair of gumboots, two new pairs of jeans and several bright sweatshirts, made her stifle her discomfort.

It assailed her again when Phillips led her into an exclusive boutique where none of the clothes had price tags, and perched himself, next to Simon, on inadequate chairs while she reluctantly modelled several outfits for them.

She was wearing the last one when she made a decision. 'None of these,' she said, with a smile at the patient saleswoman. 'They're all lovely, but they're not what I want.'

Outside, she said, 'Let's go to a fabric shop. I can buy the material and make a dress for infinitely less than you'd pay in there.'

Phillips gave her a stubborn glance, but she was tired of overbearing men forcing her to do things. 'Trust me,' she said firmly.

'Drake—' he began.

'Look, all Drake wants is for me not to look like a poor relation.' Tamping down on the sting in her tone, she said reasonably, 'I promise you, I won't. No one will know that I've made the dress.'

He didn't look convinced, but, apparently realising that this time there would be no changing her mind, made no more protests as she withdrew money from her bank account—money she no longer needed for Simon's operation—before going in search of a good fabric shop.

Both he and Simon agreed with her choice—silk velvet the exact topaz of her eyes. The price made her wince, but she comforted herself with the knowledge that it would last her for years. She'd make it medieval in style, with a body-skimming simplicity that would contrast with the rich material.

Outside, Phillips said austerely, 'You will need—ah—underclothes. The girl in the shop suggested—'

'I can't afford anything else,' she said quickly.

'Drake won't be at all happy if we go home without a complete new wardrobe for you as well as Simon.'

With more than a trace of sarcasm, she returned, 'Of course I'd like him to be happy, but not at the expense of my pride.'

Phillips directed a significant glance at Simon, who was thrusting out a foot to admire the new shoes he'd insisted on wearing out of the shop. Lowering his voice, he said, 'M—Olivia, Drake doesn't take too kindly to being thwarted. And if you don't both come home with a complete wardrobe it will simply mean more work for me, because I'll have to come back and finish the job properly.'

'He's a tyrant,' she declared. Just before they'd left the house his secretary had rung to tell her that an appointment had been made at Mirelle.

'He can be—difficult,' Phillips agreed drily.

She looked at Simon, now reverently touching the sleeve of his new anorak. 'Oh, all right,' she said, trying not to sound as though she'd been badly defeated, 'but I'll pay for it myself.'

'If you wish.'

She wondered whether there was a faint note of respect in his voice, but could see nothing in his face to indicate it.

On the way to the hairdressing salon she asked curiously, 'Where did you meet Drake?'

'On an island in the Pacific.'

'Some day,' she said wistfully, 'I'm going to have a holiday on one of those islands.'

'It wasn't one of the holiday islands. We were working.' His voice gave nothing away. 'It was a place where, if you stayed off the booze and away from the gambling dens and women and out of fights, you could make a lot of money in a short time.'

'I see.' So that explained those missing years. 'How long were you there?' she asked.

'Four years. We did a double tour of duty.'

She nodded. 'And then came away with your fortunes made.'

Phillips' mouth tightened. 'Drake did,' he said without emphasis. 'I'm afraid I wasn't able to stay away from the gambling dens.'

It seemed so unlike him to make such an admission that she turned to look at him. 'Compulsive?' she asked quietly.

'Yes. It's over now. That is, I can live from day to day without wanting to gamble. As I'm sure you know, one never really beats an addiction. One learns to cope with it. And for that, I can thank Drake. He quite literally saved my life.'

It seemed to be some sort of warning. Was Phillips nailing his colours to the mast, telling her that his loyalty was entirely to Drake? Whatever, he must think it important, to have bared his soul like that; she didn't need to look at him to know how traumatic the experience had been.

She said with patent sincerity, 'I think you're very brave and very strong to have overcome it.'

'I wouldn't have been able to do it without him.'

'Nonsense,' she retorted robustly. 'The desire had to come from you.'

He permitted himself a small, ironic smile. 'The desire to beat it was always there, but if Drake hadn't threatened to knock my block off the next time I went anywhere near a gambling den, I doubt whether it would ever have developed beyond a desire. I was thoroughly afraid of Drake—especially as I knew he meant it. He had a fearsome reputation. Not a man to be crossed.'

Yes, it was a definite warning. She looked at the traffic moving slowly down Parnell Rise. 'It seems as though time has mellowed him, then.'

'No. He expects fair play and honesty; if anyone lets him down he doesn't forget.'

Coming from Phillips, that was tantamount to saying Drake had an urge for revenge that Titus Andronicus might have envied.

The last leaves on the deciduous trees in a small park they passed were falling; most were brown and boring. Auckland's mild, humid climate was not conducive to an autumn display. Much further south at Springs Flat leaf-fall came earlier, after a season fired by torches of gold and orange and scarlet in the sunstruck paddocks.

The visit to the hairdresser might have been profoundly uncomfortable if Olivia had allowed the swiftly disguised astonishment on the face of the receptionist to affect her. As she watched her hair being cut she wondered what Drake would think of it, then hastily banished the thought.

It returned, however, when she saw the finished result. By some alchemy of skill the hairdresser had transformed her straggly locks to a honey-blonde bob. Startled, she stared at her reflection. Even with the lingering effects of the bronchitis dampening down the colour in her cheeks and lips, she looked better than she ever had.

Would Drake like it?

Having steeled herself for some comment, Olivia was perversely hurt when he didn't seem to notice.

However, over dinner that night he did ask, 'Did you buy yourself a dress for Saturday night?'

'I'm surprised you don't ask Phillips,' she snapped.

His brows lifted. 'Why should I?'

'Wasn't he told to make sure I did buy one?'

'No,' he said calmly. 'This is between you and me, Olivia. I wouldn't put him in that position.'

Ever-betraying heat ran up through her skin as she forced herself to swallow a forkful of delicious chicken. It tasted like ashes, but at least the feeling of being called to account for a pathetic piece of spite faded slightly.

The respite gave her enough composure to be able to say, 'You don't need to worry about Saturday night. I'll look sinfully expensive.'

'What else did you buy?'

She felt her mulish look come over her face and tried to conceal it. 'Underclothes,' she said reluctantly.

'I see,' he said, looking at her with enigmatic detachment. 'Finish your meal.'

'Why?'

'Because you and I are going shopping. It's late night at Newmarket. I'll make sure you have a decent wardrobe if I have to stuff you into the clothes myself.'

'Don't be silly,' she snapped, giving up any pretence of eating. Then, because the last thing she wanted to do was go shopping with him, she capitulated. 'All right, I'll go tomorrow and buy whatever I need.'

'Everything?'

She nodded mutinously.

'You weren't always so easily intimidated,' he taunted. 'Once you would have told me to do my worst and walked away with that maddening swing of your hips, daring me to do anything about it.'

'I had some freedom of choice then,' she countered, because the images his words conjured embarrassed her.

'You should have thought about that before you wrote that letter. And I don't think freedom or the lack of it made any difference to your character. Growing up might have. At seventeen you were thoroughly spoilt, convinced you were a touch above everyone else in the district.'

It was true. She had been arrogant and self-centred and imperious, enjoying her position as a social success, but it hurt to hear the words from him. 'Is that why you propositioned me last night?'

She should have looked him boldly in the eyes; instead, she buttered another piece of roll and popped it into her mouth, chewing vigorously.

'To get back at you because you were the boss's daughter and I was just the clerk's son?' A taut few moments of silence stretched unbearably until eventually he said, 'I rather think I've been insulted by an expert. Do you really believe that, Olivia?'

'I certainly *don't* believe you took one look at me when we met again and wanted me,' she said, hiding the bitterness in the words with a scornful smile. 'I have no illusions about the way I look.'

'I didn't realise you'd been brought up to believe that clothes and make-up are all that make a woman desirable.'

I was brought up by a woman so beautiful that people used to stop and stare after her in the street, she wanted to say.

She had always known that she couldn't compete with her mother. It had never worried her; she hadn't grown up feeling inferior because of it. Or not until she'd learned that her mother had slept with the man to whom she had given her virgin heart. A man who wanted Elizabeth would find nothing attractive about her daughter.

And because that thought was so unpalatable, she shrugged it away and retorted acidly, 'They help.'

'At first impression, perhaps. Of course physical beauty is important to men—perhaps more important than it is to women. But it's a stupid man who lets his gonads choose his lover or his wife.'

His frankness shocked her. She made a pretence at eating another mouthful as the infuriating colour stole back up through her skin, then said defensively, 'Well, I won't look like the wrath of God on Saturday night, anyway.'

'I'm glad to hear it,' he returned courteously.

The next day she went to Parnell on the bus and chose material for separates, shirts, skirts and trousers. By buying carefully she managed to run to two pairs of shoes and some more underwear as well—neat, plain chainstore garments, unromantic but practical. And if she did stand beside a rack of exquisite garments, silk and lace and pintucks, even lift a hand to touch them before remembering her calluses and hangnails, well, no one was there to see her do it, or to see her wistfully ironic smile as she turned away.

That afternoon she coaxed Phillips into helping her carry an old table down from the attic to her bedroom and set up her sewing machine on it; it looked distinctly plebian in the luxurious room, but she smiled with satisfaction when it was done.

Simon decided to spend the afternoon painting a garden gate with Phillips, so Olivia had peace and quiet as she cut out the silk velvet. She knew exactly how she was going to make it, and blessed her one talent—that of being able to draft patterns in her head.

It was exhilarating to work with such superb material—so exhilarating, in fact, that she was still there when someone knocked on her door.

They must have finished the gate, she thought guiltily, calling, 'Come in if you're clean.'

But neither Simon nor Phillips opened the door. Instead Drake stood there, his brows drawn together as he saw the table and the machine.

'What the hell are you doing?' he asked quietly.

'Sewing.'

The laconic answer didn't please him at all. He walked silently across the room to look down at her work. 'I told you to buy—'

'I bought the material.' Trying to mute the defiant note in her voice, she said, 'Drake, be reasonable. This is by far the cheapest way of providing myself with a wardrobe, and I really enjoy sewing.'

A lean finger touched the silk velvet, moving with sensuous lightness across the material. He said slowly, 'When will it be finished?'

'This time tomorrow. It's not closely fitted, so it's easy to make. The finishing will take a little more time, but I'll only do the most necessary stuff.' To say any more would have sounded ominously like pleading, so she buttoned down the words of justification that threatened to spill out. Ridiculous to feel that something vital was riding on this exchange—and yet that was exactly how she felt.

Grey-green eyes searched her face. She met his gaze with all of the fortitude she possessed, determined not to give in.

Finally, when her nerves were stretched to singing point, he said, 'All right, then. But I want to see it in time to buy another if it doesn't come up to scratch.'

'Very well,' she returned, through teeth clamped so tightly together that she could have bitten the words and chewed them into nothing.

His smile was one-sided and oddly sympathetic. 'It's for your own good,' he said, and left her.

On Saturday evening she donned the dress with a shameful flicker of pleasure, because it was the loveliest thing she had ever worn in her life. Amazing, she thought, what a few days of rest and comparative peace had done for her—although peace wasn't what she felt when Drake was home. His presence gave an edge to life, honed her senses so that the sky was bluer and her food more tasty, and the air whispered over her skin in a secret, forbidden caress.

And then she'd remember that Simon was the result of an adulterous affair that had killed her mother, that every horrible thing that had happened to them was the direct result of Drake's uncontrolled lust. And she'd wonder how she could react so violently to his presence when he was everything she despised.

Her hands trembled slightly as she smoothed the velvet over her hips.

Drake had spent much of the morning out, but had arrived back with a child's cricket set, and after lunch all four of them had played.

'Drake and me,' Simon decided, 'cause we're the biggest and the smallest, and you and Phillips, Liv.'

It was hot, so they all donned hats and went out onto the lowest lawn, where Drake showed his son how to set up the bails and pace out the pitch, explaining the game to him.

They were not in the least alike, she thought again, watching them as she put an insulated bag of cold drinks in the shade of the jacaranda tree. Not in looks, not in anything. For some reason—one she wasn't going to explore—she was glad of that.

With the utmost patience Drake coached Simon, showing him how to hold the bat, how to catch a ball, praising the boy without stint when he finally managed to grasp it in his still chubby hands. Simon was growing fast, she thought with an odd clutch at her heart. Last year those hands had been like starfish, but now the fingers were lengthening, and his round face was changing to reveal the structure of the man he was going to be.

Her eyes drifted up to the man showing him how to bowl. The strongly defined framework of his face was too authoritative to be handsome. The word didn't mean anything applied to Drake; he transcended the description. He was a man who had worked and taken the measure of life, who wouldn't give in, whose control and self-discipline had been earned in dangerous places.

'Come on, Liv, we're ready to start,' Simon called out bossily, tossing the ball at her.

Jerked out of her reverie, she caught it and flung it on to Phillips.

Although Olivia hadn't played cricket for years she found the skills had never left her and enjoyed herself immensely, long legs flying as she dashed between the stumps. Simon showed promise, and Phillips, for all his age and a solid build that made him look more like a boxer than an athlete, proved to be a handy batsman and a killer bowler. Drake tempered his expertise—although he got her out with ridiculous ease.

Now, bathed and dressed and desperately uncertain, her reflection still unfamiliar in the mirror, she unscrewed the top of the tube of lipstick that had been her most frivolous purchase the day before and carefully outlined her mouth.

It was peach, a deeper, more intense shade of the colour that rioted through her skin when she was embarrassed, and it set off the tawny-gold dress and the gleaming gold of her eyes perfectly. It would have to be enough because she had nothing else—no powder, no subdued colour to smooth over her eyelids—and in a few minutes she was going downstairs to be introduced, perhaps, to the woman Simon had seen kissing Drake.

Nervousness cramped her stomach. She had crept about in the shadows for so long that this emergence into a social life was terrifying. Drake had told her who was going to be there: a young couple, Mary and Rupert Watson, who were something to do with motor sports, and a PR officer in Drake's firm called Sarah Beale, as well as a couple of old friends and a man from Hawaii who was connected with tourism.

She just hoped that she wouldn't make a total fool of herself. All she knew about entertaining she had learned from her mother in that life which she sometimes thought had never really existed.

There came a knock at the door. Dragging in a deep breath, she walked over and opened it.

CHAPTER SIX

'READY?' Drake said. His grey-green eyes roved her face, fastened onto the soft fullness of her mouth for heart-shaking seconds, then began a deliberate survey of the rest of her.

Damn him, she seethed silently. He had already given his approval to the dress; he was doing this specifically to annoy and unsettle her. So angry she could feel herself shake with it, she was not going to let him see that the slow perusal was setting fire to her nerve-ends. So she lifted her head and followed suit, taking in the broad shoulders and lethal, lithe grace, the eye-pleasing blend of rugged masculinity and grace that was Drake. Her spark of defiance did nothing to ease her awareness of him.

'You look utterly charming,' he said.

'So do you,' she returned sweetly, sweeping past him and out of the room. The suspicious warmth engendered by his compliment coloured her cheeks all the way down the stairs, and she totally forgot that she had been dreading the introductions.

Much later she was to wonder whether he had known of her feelings, and had intentionally infuriated her to banish them. It didn't seem likely, but then, he was an enigma.

Olivia had expected the whole evening to be an ordeal, and an ordeal it was. What she hadn't expected was that through it all Drake would be an unobtrusive support.

Not that an ordinary person would have needed any support. The guests were pleasant, if a trifle curious, and they were not so closely linked that any outsider was made to feel an alien. She especially liked Drake's friends, a gloriously beautiful woman called Aura Jensen and her large, impressively forceful husband, Flint.

Everyone was welcoming and pleasant, yet she felt as though there was a glass wall between her and the rest of them—a wall that no one could surmount. These nice, well-dressed, well-fed people had absolutely no idea how she had spent the last five years. They had no idea what poverty was like. It didn't help to know that once she too would have been totally ignorant of the kind of life she had been leading. Now she wondered how they would react in a similar situation, how swiftly the trappings and gloss of civilisation would be stripped from them if they lost everything.

So it was as an alien that she went through the evening, neither hostess nor guest, not friend nor business acquaintance. And eroding the serene façade she tried to present was the presence of Sarah Beale, a tiny, elegant woman with a swift, not too unkind wit, a disarming gurgle of laughter and hair the colour of silver-gilt. Was she the blonde Olivia had seen in the car outside the flat—the woman who had kissed Drake the night Simon had spied from the top of the stairs? Despising herself, Olivia watched her covertly, trying to discern just how familiar she was with Drake.

Urbane and courteous, Drake treated her no differently from the rest of the women there, but although Sarah was discreet, Olivia sensed with an atavistic instinct that she was very interested in Drake.

But then, Olivia thought, apart from Aura every woman around the antique Georgian dining table responded to their host. The secret, subliminal signs of attraction were involuntary, but they were there for the discerning eye to read. The men, too, treated him with the hidden, masculine signs of respect accorded to a dominant male.

'Look at them,' Aura Jensen said in a low, amused murmur after dinner. 'Two of a kind.'

Olivia looked across the room. Completely at ease with each other, Drake and Flint were standing by the window. As she watched Drake said something and both men laughed. She understood what Aura meant. 'Lords of creation,' she said, with what she hoped was a tolerant smile.

Aura laughed softly. 'We shouldn't allow them in the same room together. They're overpowering enough by themselves, but side by side they take your breath away.' She turned her beautiful eyes onto Olivia. 'Drake tells me you and your brother are staying here,' she said.

'Yes.' How much had he told her? By the sound of it, he hadn't admitted that Simon was his son, or that he planned to have them live with them.

'Flint and I live sixty miles away, but I'm up and down to Auckland quite often. If you'd like to, we could meet for lunch.'

It was not quite the hand of friendship, although the other woman's voice was warm and her smile open. Olivia thought that Aura Jensen probably took some time to make friends, but she didn't mind such reserve; she disliked a pretence of intimacy after a couple of meetings. 'I'd like that very much,' she said, smiling.

'Good. I'll ring you.'

They were interrupted by Sarah Beale, who came across the room followed almost immediately by Drake and Flint.

'How long do you intend to stay in Auckland, Olivia?' she asked as she sat down on the sofa beside Aura. She had excellent legs, and the black chiffon dress she wore displayed their elegant length superbly, as superbly as the colour contrasted with her delicate skin and bright hair.

'She plans to go to university here.' Drake's intervention was smooth.

'That will be fun.' Sarah looked from his hard-hewn face with its bluntly chiselled angles to Olivia's. 'What will you take?'

Very aware of Drake standing behind her chair, Olivia said quietly, 'I'd thought of doing law.'

The American from Hawaii, a large man whose features proclaimed his kinship with distant Maori cousins in New Zealand, grinned. 'So you don't subscribe to Shakespeare? "Let's kill all the lawyers"...'

Olivia laughed. 'No, not entirely. You can do an awful lot of good if you're a lawyer.'

'You don't sound altogether sure of that,' Drake said.

He saw too much. She shrugged. 'I might be in the process of changing my mind.'

'There's no need to be in a hurry to make a decision; you've until next year to do that,' he returned casually. 'In the meantime you can potter around here.'

Olivia was acutely conscious of Aura's swift glance at her husband, and the way Sarah Beale froze for a moment as the delicate colour ebbed from her skin, leaving a trace of skilfully applied blusher.

Conversation became general again, but after that Olivia realised that without being obvious about it Sarah watched her closely. Had Drake chosen that way to tell them that Olivia was going to be a permanent fixture?

At last they left. Unsure of whether she should go with Drake to say goodbye, she decided that it might look too proprietorial, as though she was taking over the role of hostess. So she said goodbye in the big sitting room where they'd sat talking for half an hour or so after dinner, and began to stack the coffee-cups and saucers.

'I can do that, miss,' Phillips said, appearing in the doorway.

She jumped. 'I thought we had an agreement,' she said, 'Mr Phillips.'

He acknowledged it with a half-hidden smile. 'Old habits die hard, Olivia,' he said, deftly putting the glasses and coffee-cups onto a tray. 'You look very nice. Simon told me you looked like a princess in your new dress. He was right.'

'Simon is a bit biased,' she said, flushing at the compliment.

'I don't think so. You look very ladylike.'

Clearly this was his greatest accolade. Olivia swept a deep, formal, graceful curtsey straight from her ballet lesson days.

Phillips' brows shot up, but for the first time he smiled without the restraint she had come to think of as an integral part of his character. A milestone! Rising, she heard the soft, heavy thud of the front door shutting. Drake had walked his guests out to their cars and was now back inside. Oddly, the palms of her hands began to sweat. Taking up a position in front of a superb landscape, she gazed fixedly at it, as though the sculpted shapes of hills and islands held the key to heaven.

'Goodnight, Phillips. I'll see you in the morning.' Drake's voice sent strange little chills up and down her spine.

Phillips said, 'What time do you want breakfast?'

'Sunday is your day off.'

'I don't have anything to do until the marathon starts at ten. I might as well get breakfast.'

Olivia listened keenly. They had an unusual relationship, these two, but although they spoke formally to each other it was impossible to miss the mutual respect. So Phillips was a runner; that must be what he disappeared to do for two hours after dinner each night.

'Only if you eat it with us,' Drake said.

'You drive a hard bargain,' Phillips said, another of his rare smiles echoing in his tone. 'Goodnight.'

He left. Olivia felt Drake move across the big room to stand behind her. It was stupid to stare at a picture, but a complex and obscure shyness kept her face turned from his too-perceptive scrutiny.

'You seem to be entranced with the landscape,' he said mildly.

'It's glorious.' She hesitated, before saying in a tight voice, 'Drake, had you thought that I could turn out to be a damned nuisance to you if you want to get married?'

'I must confess I hadn't,' he said lazily, 'but I promise you I don't intend marrying in the immediate future.'

She swung around, meeting unreadable grey-green eyes. 'If you do fall in love,' she ploughed on, determined to sound matter-of-fact and confident, 'you must tell me, and I'll go. I realise that your wife wouldn't want an encumbrance like me around.'

'Had you thought,' he enquired, 'that this putative wife might not want an encumbrance like Simon around too?'

'Simon and I go together, of course; I took that for granted,' she said, adding rashly, 'You should have thought of that when you were getting my mother pregnant.'

Something moved in the dense depths of his eyes, something feral that prowled like a tiger through his controlled mastery of his emotions. 'So I should have,' he agreed. 'I assume that if you do move out you'll expect to be supported by me?'

She flinched. 'If you wait for four or five years,' she retorted, 'I'll be able to support him. It's only fair, now I come to think of it, because I'll have to wait to get married—'

'Olivia, go to bed,' he said calmly.

Feeling as though she'd narrowly missed being scorched by a vicious fire, she took herself off, thanking the pride that enabled her to walk regally from the room.

The next few days passed slowly. Olivia was unable to shake off a sense of unease; it coloured her normally equable temperament and her thoughts, and although she tried hard to overcome it, as the days shortened and the tangerine glow of winter appeared in the clear morning and evening skies, she became short-tempered and irritable, reining back her temper with a real effort.

Always before she had managed to summon some enthusiasm, a steady conviction that even when things seemed uniformly grim, hope and happiness lay somewhere ahead.

Now she looked at the life she'd led and saw it pinched by poverty, narrow and grinding and dull. Before she had justified it by telling herself that Simon's welfare was paramount, and indeed it had been. She had no regrets about her actions, she regretted merely that she had missed so much by doing what she knew to be right.

Soon she'd be twenty-five. For some reason her birthday began to symbolise all that she had lost, all that she could never attain.

Of course she blamed Drake for her mood, and of course she knew she was wrong. This didn't, however, stop her from sewing all day, and often after Simon had gone to bed—although she knew that Drake didn't like it. He was, she told herself righteously, being overbearing and arbitrary. He had no right to try and monitor her leisure activities.

It utterly infuriated her that he didn't say a word about it, even when she provoked him by hand-finishing the garments in the evenings.

Four days after the dinner party she was sitting under the jacaranda, sewing tiny white buttons on a blouse in the late afternoon sunlight, when the sound of a vehicle brought her head up. A taxi was moving slowly along the drive.

Setting the garment down, she got to her feet and walked over, only to stop with her hand pressed to her heart as the passenger got out and paid. She knew instantly who it was: Brian Harley. Her stepfather.

The blood drained from Olivia's skin. It was a cliché she had read a hundred times, but that was exactly what it felt like, leaving her cold and clammy and terrified. Her hands shook until she gripped them tightly together; she gaped at the man who walked so arrogantly towards her, grey head gleaming in the sunlight, as though she had just seen a ghost.

Another cliché, she thought, trying desperately to distance herself from this, but just as true. Of course, that was why they were clichés—because they were all true.

The taxi waited, its engine purring quietly. *Simon*, she thought, her brain jangling.

No, he was all right; he was with Phillips in the kitchen. She would stay here.

'Hello, Olivia,' Brian Harley said, gazing at her with gloating eyes. 'I always knew you'd turn up sooner or later.'

Why hadn't people realised that he was mad?

'What do you want?' she asked huskily, refusing to look away, meeting his eyes with forced composure.

'I came for my son,' he said, smiling.

She stared at him. 'You haven't got a son.'

A queer smile hardened on his thin lips. 'His birth certificate says I have.'

This man had made her mother's life hell. He would do the same to Simon until, like his mother, he became an automaton in order to survive. Or until he cracked and shattered.

Although her pounding heart almost drowned out the sound of her voice, she said evenly, 'There is no way you're going to get your hands on Simon, so you've come on a wild-goose chase.'

His smile widened. 'Don't be so stupid,' he said confidently. 'No court would deny a father his son.'

She said intensely, 'He is not your son. And I can prove it.'

'How?'

What she still thought of as his cat-and-mouse look was on his face now, filling her with the revulsion and fear it had always aroused. It should have helped to remind herself that he no longer possessed any power over her, but somehow it didn't.

'DNA,' she said succinctly. 'He's been tested.'

'Indeed?' He smiled with a scary mixture of pity and amusement. 'Then I'd better get my solicitor to demand the results of the test.' He paused. 'He can do that when he's suing for custody of my legal heir, and seeing the police about a kidnapping.'

He turned and walked back across the grass towards the waiting taxi, leaving Olivia witless and shaking.

Ten minutes later she was still standing there, so lost in panic-stricken terror that when Drake drove up the drive she didn't move, didn't even realise that he'd stopped the car and come striding across the grass.

'What's happened? What's going on?' he asked harshly.

Shuddering, her eyes glazed with tears she didn't dare shed, she said, 'My stepfather came. I *told* you he'd find us! I *told* you I shouldn't be seen—'

'Stop that this minute!' He took her by the shoulders and shook her—not fiercely, just enough to jolt her out of her horror-induced trance. 'All right, what did he say?'

'That he's suing for custody of Simon. He wants the results of the DNA test and he threatened me with prosecution for kidnapping.'

Searching for reassurance, she looked up at him, but could read nothing in his face.

'Go on. What else did he say?'

She told him as well as she could remember, finishing hopelessly, 'He'll take Simon away and he'll hurt him so badly he'll ruin him—just as he did my mother. I saw what he did to her—he's an expert at psychological warfare. He made her life so miserable that she died rather than live like that.' Her eyes focused on his face with its austere features bluntly delineated into a mask of strength. Through her teeth she said, 'You abandoned her to hell! I'll never forgive you for that! Oh, God, what can we do? He—'

'Calm down. He won't take him away,' Drake said with such iron-clad control that she almost believed him.

Only for a second, however. 'It's all your fault,' she said, the hot words homing through the quiet, grass-scented air like missiles. 'Why couldn't you have left her alone? They had a reasonable sort of marriage—'

'If they had a reasonable marriage,' he said brusquely, 'she wouldn't have been seduced, would she? Now, shut up—I have to think.'

He let her go and stood, dark head held high, hands thrust into his trouser pockets so that the expensive material was stretched across his thighs.

An idea sprang full-blown into her head. Without thinking of the consequences, she blurted, 'Drake, we'll have to get married.'

'Married?' he said slowly. Beneath their heavy lids his eyes were opaque, unreadable. 'Why?'

'Because if we're married we avoid any suggestion of immorality—I don't know whether that weighs with a family court judge, but a stable marriage would.'

'A stable home with plenty of money.' His voice was dry. 'Go on.'

'Well, if it comes to a court case, possession is nine points of the law, isn't it?'

'If the possessor was the only mother the child had ever had, it probably would be.'

'Especially if we seemed to be happily married,' she said eagerly.

'For how long?'

'What?'

'How long will we stay married?'

She flushed, realising just what she was expecting of him. However, determination and an implacable protectiveness overrode her qualms. 'I—well, until Simon is old enough to tell the court where he wants to live.'

'Six years, give or take a few years. And what sort of marriage would this be?' he asked coolly. 'An exercise in futility, or a real one?'

Colour washed over her skin. She said with difficulty, 'If you want it to be a real one—'

'Oh, spare me the noble offer!' His voice was caustic and contemptuous. 'I'm not into necrophilia, Olivia.'

She flinched and he asked on a note of mockery, 'Changing your mind?'

She shook her head. 'No,' she said, relinquishing her barely formed fantasy of marriage as a communion of mind and spirit as well as body. She continued passionately, 'Simon is the most important person in the world to me, and I won't let my stepfather get his hands on him.'

'All right.'

Her jaw dropped. Faintly she demanded, 'All right, what?'

'All right, we'll get married. I'll organise it. I wonder how he knew you were here.'

She looked up to meet eyes that were unexpectedly keen and hard. 'Somebody told him. You know how gossip flies.'

'Not that fast. Not unless he was already looking for you. And if that was so, I wonder why he wants the boy.'

'I told you before—he wants revenge.'

Drake's mouth took on a sardonic curve. 'Do you really think he'd go to all this trouble and expense— because it's going to cost him megabucks—just for that? He can't hurt Elizabeth any more, and why should he hate you?'

'He sacked your father, remember? That was pure, spiteful revenge—because he couldn't hurt you.'

'Yes, I know. Actually, to a certain extent I can understand that. No man—' he held up his hand as she went to speak '—enjoys being a cuckold. I said I understand it, not that I condone it. This melodramatic, wicked squire routine, however, doesn't ring quite true.'

'You don't know him,' she said, shivering.

'I probably know him better than you do,' he said with a smile that lifted the hairs on the back of her neck. 'You're cold. Get into the car and I'll take you up.'

The sun had set, and the crisp air was settling damply on her bare arms. Olivia picked up her needlework, oddly grateful that she had been sewing on the last button when her stepfather arrived, and accompanied Drake across the short grass of the lawn to the waiting car. Marrying him was like setting out onto a hazardous sea with no prospect of rescue, but it was the only thing to do. And if it meant that they both had to give up dreams—well, she'd had plenty of practice at that, and it was time Drake learnt what it was like.

Which was petty of her. His injury and his manager's crime had deprived him of his career.

As the car swept up through shrubberies and lawns towards the gracious house Olivia slanted a glance across at his decisive profile, with its straight nose and resolute angle of jaw and chin. Hastily, because something febrile and uncontrollable stirred in the pit of her stomach, she looked away.

'It's going to be all right,' Drake murmured as the garage door came down behind them. 'Don't panic; just leave everything to me.'

It would be perilously easy to do just that—easy, and dangerous.

'I'll have to buy some more material to make up,' she said inanely. 'I can't wear the velvet dress—' And she stopped, as a sudden, appalled understanding of what she'd done struck her.

In the shadows of the immaculate garage she saw his unpleasant smile. 'It was your idea. Look at it this way,' he drawled, switching off the engine, 'when we're married I hand over all my worldly goods to you in church, and at least half of them legally. I don't think a wedding dress is going to make much of a dent in them. I'm a comparatively rich man.'

Her voice sounded oddly loud in the silent garage. 'I don't want your money—not any of it! Get your lawyer to write a marriage contract and I'll sign it.'

'An excellent idea,' he said urbanely, turning towards her.

Before she had time to realise what he intended, his hand caught the heavy fall of hair at the back of her neck, tilting her face to meet his. For a few seconds they looked at each other, Olivia's eyes widening in the dimness.

Hard, she thought in confusion; his face was blunt and resolute and unyielding, the features combining to proclaim a strength that wasn't in the least negated by the curly black lashes that half covered his eyes. But beneath those lashes his eyes gleamed pure green, icy yet exciting, the sensual glitter unnerving and stimulating.

Olivia tried to summon antagonism to meet and match his obvious intention, but although it seethed through her brain, her body recognised a deeper, sharper need, and capitulated.

Her mouth dried. When she touched her tongue to her lips a flame melted the ice in his eyes.

And then his head lowered. Something inexorable about the kiss branded her right down to the foundations of her soul. Although she resented it she couldn't resist, because her body was held in thrall by a response older than time, older than thought.

Even as she wondered confusedly why she had no defences he overwhelmed her. She drowned in the scent of him, in the taste of his mouth, in the soft abrasion of his lips, the firm way his hand held her head still, long fingers sliding through the thick silk of her hair as though he reacted as violently to her as she did to him.

It was like being taken over by an alien, she thought, a faint, rational part of her brain trying to order the experience, catalogue it and file it. She had nothing to compare it with, nothing but his other kisses, and this one was different.

Much later she would recognise that difference, and be able to categorise it as possessiveness. But at this moment she was too lost in a primitive carnality to comprehend, let alone be able to classify. As his mouth crushed hers she murmured softly and opened her lips beneath his insistent seeking. Hot shivers surged through her; she strained towards him, wanting so much more than a kiss yet too unsure of herself to know what to do. His arm tightened around her; the heavy beat of his heart against her breasts increased her feverish tension.

Just when she was beginning to get frightened he lifted his head and looked down at her, that enigmatic mouth curved in cool satisfaction.

'So, we've sealed our pact in the time-honoured way,' he said, letting her go. 'We'd better tell the other members of our household.'

It was, of course, impossible to discern what Phillips really thought, although he offered his congratulations. For some reason Simon was wary.

'Will I have to call you Uncle Drake?' he asked, looking from Olivia's face to that of the man beside her.

'No. Why?'

His thin shoulders moved. 'I just like calling you Drake,' he muttered.

Drake ruffled his hair lightly. 'That's all right. I hear you're going to the hospital tomorrow.'

Simon straightened. 'Yes,' he said importantly. 'I have to get grommets put in my ears so I can hear properly.

Then I can go back to school. What school will I be going to?'

'There's a school just down the road,' Drake said casually.

Simon nodded, then with apparent uninterest asked, 'Can I watch television?'

Olivia shook her head. Opening his mouth to protest, Simon glanced at Drake and without demur resigned himself to the inevitable. 'Well, can you teach me how to play chess, then, Drake? Phillips said you're the best chess player in the whole world.'

Watching them as they sat over a chessboard, Olivia felt something break in the region of her heart. She tried not to be resentful of Simon's burgeoning adoration for his father, telling herself that only a mean-spirited person would think it unfair.

She should be glad that Drake liked his son, and seemed to know almost intuitively how to deal with him. From the first he had pitched his voice so that Simon could hear him clearly, and treated him with a calm patience that was exactly what Simon needed.

She was glad. Only—well, it did seem unfair!

Shelving that unprofitable subject, she began to worry about her stepfather's chances of getting custody. Later in the evening, when she jumped up for the fourth time to see where Simon was, Drake said, 'Stop being so jittery. He's cutting a cabbage for dinner with Phillips.'

'I know I'm being silly,' she said, watching Phillips and Simon come across the back lawn, Simon almost staggering under the weight of a huge cabbage, 'but I can't help wondering whether my stepfather might not decide for himself that possession is nine points of the law.'

'He might, but Phillips isn't going to let anything happen to Simon—and neither am I. And although your stepfather might want him, he's an idiot if he puts a foot out of line. No court would give custody to a man who kidnapped a child from the only mother he can remember.'

'He's not an idiot,' Olivia said in a low voice, relaxing as Simon's laughter echoed down the hall. She hesitated, then added, 'But I don't think he's sane. Not about this, anyway.'

'Are you sure you're not overreacting?'

'No!'

He said quietly, 'He didn't kill your mother, Olivia.'

'How do you know?'

'I requested a copy of the inquest findings and a transcript of the evidence. It came today. The doctor was quite sure that her injury was caused by the edge of the table. They found where she'd actually hit her head on it. Your stepfather stated that she'd been ill and hadn't eaten that day.'

'She'd had a mild stomach bug,' she said.

'So she would have been unsteady on her feet. He said he'd helped her into bed and that she was almost asleep when he left her to go to his own room. The medical evidence supported his testimony, so it was presumed that she'd got up in the middle of the night and fainted and hit her head on the corner of the table. There was no sign of any other blow.'

Shivering, she noted the wide, hard, arrogantly outlined mouth, the indefinable air of toughness that was as much a part of him as the grey-green eyes and those tilted brows, the olive skin and blunt, formidable features. If anyone could keep Simon safe, she thought, Drake could.

His eyes raked her white face. He said, 'Or is there something else—something you haven't told me?'

Tension sharpened her voice. 'No.'

He got to his feet and came across and took her hands. 'Did he abuse you, Olivia?' he asked quietly.

She shook her head. 'No, never. I always knew he didn't like me much, but he was just—distant. He used to taunt Mother,' she went on slowly, 'after you left. And when he'd reduced her to tears he'd look like that— smugly triumphant, yet sneering. I saw that look again today and it reminded me.'

'And you immediately regressed to being the helpless girl you were while it was all happening,' he said. 'You're no longer without support, Olivia, and you have grown up considerably since then. Don't go to pieces.'

'No, all right,' she muttered, feeling bereft as he let her hands go, but comforted by his calm decisiveness.

That night, after she'd checked Simon to make sure that he was asleep in his room, Drake said, 'Would you mind coming along to my office for a moment?'

She hadn't been there before. It was a big room lined by bookshelves, part library, part very up-to-date office, equipped with a facsimile machine and computer on a huge desk. Like its owner, it looked efficient and organised and disciplined.

Drake waited until she was seated before handing her a piece of paper. 'Would you like to fill this in?'

A quick glance revealed that he intended to open a bank account for her. Olivia straightened her spine, hiding her instinctive revulsion at the idea. It was only pragmatic, she realised, and in a way she had earned it. She had cared for his son while he was out setting up the business that provided the money. And the unemployment benefit would stop as soon as she married.

Nevertheless, she hated accepting it. Writing hastily, she filled in the particulars.

'Thank you,' she said stiffly, handing it back.

'It's nothing.'

An undertone of—what? Amusement? Perhaps, but if there was humour there it was shaded by another, less discernible emotion. Her quick, proud glance was unable to find anything in his face but a grave, impersonal interest. He wore a mask, she thought, a mask made of mirrors, so that instead of his face revealing his thoughts it reflected hers back at her.

'I've drafted out a marriage contract; read it and tell me if you agree with it.'

'I don't need—'

Holding out the sheet of paper, he interrupted crisply, 'Olivia, for once just shut up and read it. It was, after all, your idea!'

Subsiding, she obeyed. The notes stipulated the allowance he planned to give her—an enormous amount, she thought worriedly—with provisions for increasing it if necessary. Drake would also make himself responsible for her university fees. In return, she would care for Simon as though she were his mother, live wherever Drake wanted her to, and at all times behave as his wife.

The marriage was to last until Simon reached the age of thirteen. If either wished to divorce after that she would not oppose equal access to Simon. Drake would pay Simon's expenses and provide accommodation for them both in a suitable environment, but that would be the extent of his financial support.

It didn't seem right that divorce should be foreseen with such cold-blooded detachment, but then, this wasn't a normal marriage. 'That's a huge allowance,' she said doubtfully.

'You'll buy all your clothes with it.' Again that equivocal note in his tone.

'All right,' she said, giving him back the paper.

'I'll get my solicitor to turn it into a legal document,' he said indifferently, putting it on the desk. 'And I'll organise a solicitor for you too.'

'I don't need a solicitor.'

His broad shoulder lifted. Very drily he said, 'You do. It would be too easy for someone to say that I took advantage of your naïvety and persuaded you to sign an agreement that was detrimental to your financial interests.'

The comment stung, as it had been meant to. The two thousand dollars he had paid to Brett danced in front of her eyes. 'I wouldn't do that!'

'I'm sure you wouldn't,' he said gently, but there was a cool gleam in his eyes that told her he didn't believe her.

It hurt that he didn't trust her. She almost gave in to it, but instantly caught herself up. What did it matter? The important thing was Simon's security; that, after all, was why they were both taking this vast step into the unknown.

'By the way,' he said casually, 'have you still got the miniature?'

He had turned away to put the paper in a thin black leather briefcase, so all she could see was the blunt determination of his profile.

'Yes,' she acknowledged, with a reluctance that surprised her.

'I'd like to have a look at it, if I may.'

Nodding, she got to her feet, not unhappy at being given the chance to leave.

The miniature was nestled in her drawer; Olivia looked at the aristocratic young face so perceptively delineated, and thought with a flash of insight, I'll bet the man who painted this was in love with you. The sweetly imperious face gazed serenely back, and for a fragment of a second she thought that the eighteenth-century woman dressed in her finery of silk and lace smiled with wry sympathy from within the oval compass of the frame.

Whoever the artist was, Olivia thought as she turned to the door, he was brilliant. And I wonder how I could have forgotten so completely about you...

She didn't want to hand her over to the man who waited for her, but she couldn't think of a good reason for saying that she'd changed her mind. Nevertheless, an immense reluctance made her hand feel leaden, and it was all she could do not to snatch the dainty, delicate lady back.

'Painted on ivory,' he said, turning it over in his long fingers.

'How can you tell?'

'By the luminous, glowing look. The artist's used transparent water-colours so that the ivory shines through.'

'Are you an expert?'

'No,' he said absently. 'I do know a bit about them.'

'I wonder who she was?'

'Someone's ancestor, I imagine.' Eyes that were suddenly cold and searching went from the exquisite little painted face to hers. 'She's valuable. If you needed money so desperately, why didn't you sell her?'

For some reason Olivia felt naked, pilloried. 'I just forgot about her. I was astounded when Simon came out with her that night.' She knew it sounded unbelievable, and didn't blame him for his raised brows. 'Perhaps it was something deep and Freudian, because Mother so desperately wanted Simon to have her.'

'Even when you *desperately* needed the money?'

She met the painted gaze and felt a strange, swift communion with the woman in the painting. 'Yes,' she said, feeling as though she had betrayed both the unknown woman and her mother. 'She would have been the last resort.'

'How fortunate that you found another resort before the last,' he said smoothly.

Antagonism spiked her glance. 'Don't you think men should take responsibility for their children?' she enquired, sugar-sweet. 'Actually, from the way my mother spoke of it, I thought you'd given it to her. As a love token.'

His eyes held hers. 'I didn't give it to her,' he said evenly. 'And, yes, I do believe that men should take responsibility for their children. That's why you and Simon are here now; that's why we're getting married as soon as possible. Let's get one thing straight, however. I don't care what your mother told you, but I did not know that she was pregnant when I left that year.'

She wanted to believe him so much that she could taste the need in her mouth. But when she nodded he knew that she was lying, and the green-grey eyes darkened into turbulence, the colour of waves tossed by a winter storm.

'I'll put this in the safe,' he said shortly.

It was the logical thing to do with the pretty thing, but Olivia had to bite back a protest. Instead she said quietly, 'I want a receipt.'

He put the miniature down on the desk, and without looking at her leaned over and took a sheet of paper. She watched as he wrote, avoiding his eyes when he handed it to her. Her impetuous demand, born of an obscure need to hurt, had been a massive mistake, but she didn't trust him any more than he trusted her.

CHAPTER SEVEN

DRAKE took them to the hospital the next morning. It was alarmingly good to have him there. If she hadn't been so grateful, Olivia thought drily, when a single word from him called an excited, noisy Simon to heel, she might have been a little resentful of the effortless authority he wielded.

Throughout the long, exhausting day he was patient and supportive. It would, she thought on the way home, as she sat with a remarkably bouncy Simon in the back of the car, have been hell without him.

And therein lay danger. It would be far too easy to let herself learn to rely on his strength and presence. She had to remember that their marriage was to be one of pragmatism and convenience. Oh, she wasn't too inexperienced to appreciate that passion could be part of the bargain, but not respect, or love.

She knew what she was going into—a mirror marriage, reflecting only what they wanted it to, two-dimensional and shallow. Stroking a tender finger down the curve of Simon's cheek, she took a deep breath as her heart ached with inexplicable pain. It was the only way to protect Simon; she should, she thought bleakly, be happy because Simon was getting his chance.

It just showed how contrary emotion could be...

That evening, after he had finally surrendered to sleep, a ring at the door announced a visitor.

To Olivia's astonishment Phillips showed in a jeweller, accompanied by a security man who carried what looked to be a sturdy briefcase shackled to his arm.

127

'I thought you'd rather choose your rings here,' Drake said quietly.

Rings. She hadn't even thought about rings. Wishing fervently that she had organised a manicure, she nodded.

'I thought of canary diamonds to match your eyes,' Drake said. 'They've brought both modern and older settings.'

There were no prices, but even so the moment the case was opened she realised that the rings were very valuable. Her startled gaze flew to Drake, but there was no help to be found there; he wore his poker-face.

Biting her lip, she wondered whether the dark ones, gleaming like golden stars, were more expensive than the lighter, more delicate colours. It seemed ridiculous to spend a huge amount of money on a ring that symbolised nothing but a convenient arrangement.

'What's the matter?' Drake asked, holding her restless hand in his for a moment.

Surprised by his unexpected touch, she kept her eyes on the glittering array of jewels and stammered, 'I—I can't choose.'

'It's not like you to be so indecisive,' he said, his voice low and tenderly amused—for all the world, she thought with a swift flash of indignation, as though he were a real lover instead of a fake. 'All right, let's work by a process of elimination, shall we? Which ones don't you like?'

He was gentle, but inexorable, so that eventually the only ring left was one set with a magnificent stone like a sunburst, the intense colour as brilliant as the heart of a star, set off by the glitter of white diamonds along the shoulders.

'Perfect,' Drake said. 'The exact shade of your eyes.'

Oh, he was an excellent actor, no doubt about it. He didn't drool over her, or even touch her after that first brief, reassuring handclasp, but his eyes lingered on her face with unmistakable heat, and the two men would go away convinced that he couldn't wait to marry her.

'And the wedding ring?' the jeweller suggested, smiling discreetly.

That was easy. Olivia indicated a simple plain gold hoop, surprised to see that Drake chose one too, exactly the same as hers but wider.

And then the men were gone, and Drake was slipping the engagement ring onto her finger. 'An excellent choice,' he said.

'I won't dare wear it,' she said.

'You'll wear it.' He held her fingers, turning them this way and that so that the stone caught the light from the lamps and refracted it back in myriad shades and graduations of gold, from the palest lemon to a hue so intense that she had to blink and look away.

'It's beautiful,' she said, hiding a sigh.

Not well enough, however, for he said instantly, 'Don't you want to go through with it?'

Wide-eyed with shock, she looked up, and he said with a slightly twisted smile, 'No, for Simon's welfare you'd do anything—even marry a man you don't love and don't trust. Right, is there anything we haven't organised?'

She shook her head. He smiled and lifted her hand to his mouth. 'There,' he said, kissing the palm and then the back of it, his mouth warm and decisive.

The kiss, somehow intensely symbolic, pierced her heart. When he let her hand go she dithered, wondering whether she should reciprocate. It seemed churlish not to make some sort of response, especially after his graceful gesture. Suddenly making up her mind, she leaned over and kissed his cheek. For a heart-stopping moment she felt the rough silk of his skin beneath lips that tingled with an abrupt, feverish anticipation.

Hastily she pulled away and blurted the first thing that came into her mind. 'Have you heard from my stepfather?'

'No,' he said, dark brows lifting. 'Nothing at all.'

'Good,' she said, jumping to her feet. 'I think I'll go to bed now—it's been a long day.'

'Of course.' He rose with automatic courtesy, but when she reached the door he said cryptically, 'One of these days, Olivia, you're going to have to deal with this habit you've developed.'

'What habit?' she asked involuntarily.

'Running away.'

She hesitated for a betraying moment before deciding that it was safest to ignore his comment, but she heard him laugh as she closed the door behind her.

The following morning he insisted on leaving an extremely cheerful Simon in Phillips' care for the morning while he drove her to the office of the solicitor he recommended.

Of course he found a parking spot right outside the new, expensive-looking suite of offices and shops. If Drake wanted an empty car park the street wouldn't dare be crowded. Turning the key, he said, 'I'll wait here for you.'

'You don't have to,' she said. 'I can take a bus home—don't you need to go to work?'

'I'll use the phone in the car,' he said. 'Don't worry, Olivia, I won't bankrupt us. Simon is quite secure.'

Ignoring the quiver of pain his cynicism called forth, she climbed out of the car and went in.

The solicitor tried very hard to persuade her not to sign the marriage contract, or at the very least to insist on some division of property gained during the marriage, but she refused. Drake owed his son, but that responsibility didn't extend to her. Signing it quickly, she smiled at the man who clearly thought that she was mad, and emerged to find the car still there and Drake waiting.

But he didn't take her home. Instead, he drove her into town and took her to a designer's salon.

'I don't want to go here!' she whispered when she realised where they were going.

Long fingers firm around her elbow, he looked down at her with a glint of speculation. 'Tough, darling. You need clothes, and you need them now.'

'I'm making clothes—'

'And very nice they are too, for wearing around the house.' Mockery coloured the words, but beneath it was uncompromising determination.

'Even if you buy them I won't wear them,' she threatened.

His smile was lazy yet challenging. 'You'll wear them, because if you don't I'll dress you myself.' The note in his voice and the hard authority of his expression warned her that he meant what he said.

Short of making a scene, there was nothing she could do. Fuming, she allowed him to escort her into a salon decorated in chic black and white, the only splash of colour a huge ikebana arrangement of tawny chrysanthemums and canna leaves set in a bronze pot on a square of smooth white pebbles.

When the assistant showed them to a smaller private showroom Drake went too, taking the chair he was offered and stretching his long legs in front of him in a manner that indicated to Olivia, prickly with rage and frustration, how very familiar he was with such surroundings.

He didn't seem to mind waiting while the designer, a cheerful middle-aged woman improbably called Sam, and her assistant buttoned, pinned and tacked Olivia into a variety of garments before pushing her through the curtains to model for him. He looked, she thought mutinously, just like a sultan of old, making sure that the latest recruit to the harem was dressed in a manner that appealed most to his tired libido.

Except that no sultan would have watched her with such amused, ironic understanding.

Although she tried to stay aloof and silent, she couldn't be rude, and wouldn't have been human if she hadn't enjoyed the chance to try on exquisite clothes, superbly made and finished.

She tried to save face by stubbornly refusing to express any preference, but it made no difference—Drake chose, and did it with an unerring eye for what suited her best. Infuriated, she could feel the rampant curiosity seething through the designer and her offsider.

After an hour or so Drake said, 'Well, that seems to cover everything. Is there anything else you want, darling?'

It was a direct challenge.

Olivia responded immediately and without thought. Her limpid gaze met his as, smiling sweetly, she simpered, 'No thank you, darling, you've been more than generous.'

Laughter glinted in the depths of his eyes but his mouth remained firmly under control. 'Then I'll go and organise things out front.'

'Traditional, isn't he?' Sam said with a smile when he'd gone. 'Right, here's what I picked for your wedding dress. Drake said he thought you'd probably prefer something not particularly formal, but if you don't like it there are several others that would look great on you.'

It was ivory silk, a slender dream of a thing with wide shoulders and a softly draped skirt, and it fitted her perfectly. Olivia looked at it in silence. Nothing could have suited her better, and there was no way she could produce something as lovely as this.

'Oh, damn,' she said quietly, knowing that he had won.

'Don't you like it?'

Her eyes filled with tears. She said huskily, 'It's a miracle, and you know it.'

'Well, I must admit that when he described you— golden, he said you were, like something rare and precious in ivory—I thought of this straight away.' Sam stopped and looked at her. 'Tears?' she asked in quite a different tone.

Olivia sniffed. 'It's just that—my mother's dead, and I wish she could see me in this.'

It was partly true. And it worked. Sam's face instantly softened. 'I know how you feel,' she said, giving Olivia a careful hug. 'But don't you dare cry onto that beautiful silk—you'll make marks on it.'

Olivia hiccupped and laughed, and allowed herself to be helped out of it. Drake had thought of everything. There were satin shoes the same colour as the dress and a silk rose that tucked into her hair, as well as delicate stockings and underwear, a whole wardrobe of it—the sort of silk and lace and ribbons she hadn't even dared to touch a few days before. The sort of fragile luxuries a man might buy for his mistress...

Numbly, Olivia was fitted for several sets.

'I'll get those alterations done as soon as I can,' Sam said, looking satisfied. 'The wedding dress and the clothes that only need minor alterations will be ready tomorrow afternoon. I'll bring them out to the house myself, all right? The others will take a couple more days, but Drake says there's no urgency for them.'

Outside in the car Olivia said tonelessly, 'Thank you.'

'Save your thanks,' he advised sardonically. 'Why are you so sulky? Why don't you want me to buy clothes for you?'

She wouldn't look at him. 'Because it makes so much more for me to pay you back,' she snapped.

'I told you to forget about paying me back. The last five years wipe out any debts between you and me. I don't believe you, anyway. I think you're so adamant because you're afraid that whenever I look at you from now on,' he said, unerringly hitting the source of her tension right on the head, 'I'll say to myself, I bought what she's wearing next to her skin. I clothed her nakedness. Will that drive you mad, Olivia?'

You know it will, you swine, she thought, at once incensed and excited by the note of lazy sensuality in his deep voice. Aloud, she said, 'No, why should it? You're forcing me to accept them. As everyone knows, a forced action can't be held against one.' And, because she was desperate to change the subject, she countered, 'You seemed very familiar with the fashion salon. Spent a lot of time in them, have you?'

'Are you accusing me of buying clothes for a whole string of women?' he said blandly. 'I know Sam because I backed her when she needed money. As for women, there have been some, but not many—and I can assure you I don't have any perversions, or a communicable disease.'

Colour heated her skin. 'Neither do I,' she parried.

He nodded. 'So now we know where we are,' he said calmly.

Sam arrived the next afternoon with the clothes, and another woman in tow who turned out to be a cosmetician. She showed Olivia how to apply make-up, spending almost two hours with her, to Simon's interest and amazement.

He seemed perfectly recovered from the operation, but that afternoon he was more than happy to lie on the window-seat and watch and draw racing cars. The surgeon had told them that his hearing might take a while to improve, so Olivia wasn't expecting miracles straight away, but even so she thought that he seemed to be picking up conversation far more clearly than previously.

The surgeon had also told them that most children exhibited a big improvement in behaviour, which with any luck would mean an end to the tantrums. Before Drake's arrival on the scene they had been arriving more and more frequently.

It had all been worth it and, because Drake had made it happen, Olivia didn't object to the crash course in grooming. Part of her armour as Drake's wife would be the ability to blend into his world. It should be easy, because once it had been her world too, although she hadn't been old enough to understand all its rituals and mores. The years since had made her self-conscious and a little concerned about her capacity to adapt.

So she watched carefully as she was given a complete make-up.

'Fabulous skin,' the woman said appreciatively. 'And great bones too. Where did they come from?'

'My mother was breathtaking,' Olivia told her.

'Wait until I finish this. You'll be breathtaking yourself,' the woman said confidently.

It wasn't exactly the word she would have used for herself, but, abetted by the new hairstyle, the cosmetics made her look infinitely better than the defeated woman who had sat at her table only a few weeks before and wondered whether she should write to Drake Arundell.

Olivia took an intelligent interest in the process, asked questions and tried various 'looks', and obediently accepted the array of highly expensive cosmetics and skin-care products both women considered necessary.

That night, after Simon had gone to bed, Drake said, 'There's something I need to talk to you about, Olivia.'

She looked enquiringly at him, noting that his brows were drawn together as though he wasn't quite sure how to proceed. Instantly alert, Olivia sat on the edge of her chair.

His eyes were opaque, all green drained from them so that they were a wintry grey. He said, 'Before we get married we should talk about your mother.'

'No,' she said explosively, jumping to her feet.

His eyes narrowed. 'Listen—'

He was going to tell her about that long-past affair and she couldn't bear it. With a brutal lack of finesse she interrupted, 'Leave it. Our marriage is just a convenient arrangement; you don't have to tell me any of the gory details about your affair with my mother. You took advantage of a bitterly unhappy woman, and nothing you can say will make me feel anything but contempt for the way you behaved.'

'Olivia—'

'Leave it!' she said violently. 'If you must know, it makes me feel sick even to *think* of what you did. No excuses or explanations will ever give her back her life or me the years I spent clearing up the mess you left behind you. *I don't want to hear anything about it.*'

For the space of three heartbeats his gaze raked her face. Then he said calmly, 'In that case, there's nothing else for me to say.'

That night for some reason she wept herself to sleep.

She and Drake were married in a register office with Phillips and the Jensens as witnesses. Dressed in a smart new suit, Simon, who had decided over the past few days that he approved of the marriage, gave her away. He held Olivia's hand very firmly for the entire ceremony—

'Possibly,' she said to Drake as they drove back to the house afterwards, 'to make sure I wouldn't run away!'

Drake smiled ironically. 'I like that dress,' he said. 'You look enchanting.'

'Like a cheerleader.' She couldn't prevent the bite in her tone.

He laughed softly. 'What have you got against cheerleaders? They're American icons.'

'You weren't being complimentary when you said I looked like one.'

'No. But I am now. You look like everything a man would want in his new bride.'

Flattered yet wary, she locked her gaze onto the ivory silk flowing over her lap. 'Thank you,' she said. An obscure impulse persuaded her to add, 'You look very handsome too.'

'I doubt if anything could make me look that,' he said gravely, 'but it's obscurely encouraging to know that you think I can approach it.'

She directed a sharp glance his way, but although he was smiling there was little or no mockery in it. Opening her mouth to tell him that of course he was handsome, she hesitated, then closed it again without speaking.

Viewed dispassionately, he probably wasn't, but everything about him—from the blunt strength of his features to the easy masculine grace of his predator's stride, the well-made, superbly proportioned body and the way he wore his clothes with a kind of careless arrogance—combined with his intangible air of compelling, restrained authority to make him stand out in any crowd.

He had always been like that. He had blazed through quiet, sedate, conservative Springs Flat like a comet, dangerously close to consuming the little town in the restless fires of his ambition. Now the destructive compulsions that had eventually been her mother's downfall were not so visible, but Olivia knew that they were there still, merely banked and controlled.

Which was why the secret shimmer of awareness that honed her reactions, like the gold edge to pages in old books, was so dangerous.

Without volition, Olivia looked over her shoulder. Simon was absorbed in the book Drake had brought home for him the previous evening, so there was no one to fill the uneasy little hiatus in the conversation. Finally Olivia said, 'Aura looked magnificent, didn't she? I like her very much. Well, I like them both, although Flint is not easy to know.'

'He's hard,' he said calmly, 'and has no gift for instant intimacy, but, like Aura, he's loyal and honest. You couldn't ask for better friends. I've known Flint for years. He married Aura four or five years ago and they own a vineyard north of Auckland. It's Flint's dream to make a wine as good as the best Bordeaux. If anyone can do it he will.

'They're well matched. Aura is a brilliant business-woman and publicity person. They launched the first vintage last year, and sold every last bottle except the ones they've cellared for their own use. It's now getting extremely good press worldwide. At the moment they're anxiously cosseting this year's vintage.'

'She's very beautiful,' she said.

'Like a dark, glowing flame.' His voice was appreciative, but not envious.

Insensibly cheered, Olivia added, 'And he's got terrific presence. Do they have a family?'

'A son and a daughter, about four and two. Nice kids.'

And they were patently, obviously in love. Not that they flaunted it, but you could always tell, Olivia thought pensively, by the way people looked at each other, the way they moved together, the little secret, subliminal signals that revealed so much.

So if she and Drake were to pull this off they'd have to pretend like professional actors. Foreboding smeared the sparkling day.

'Do they know why we married?' she asked carefully. Simon was now humming tunefully, but she knew he could pick up odd fragments of conversation and reproduce them at the most inopportune moments.

'No.' He slanted a glance at her. 'I'd trust both of them with my life, but the more people who know, the more likely the truth is to get out—and if that happens your stepfather is going to have a much easier time convincing a judge that he has a right to access, if not custody.'

'I don't plan to tell anyone.'

'Good.'

Neither his voice nor his demeanour changed, but she looked across. 'You've heard something, haven't you?'

'Your stepfather's applied for custody of his son.'

'He is *not* his son,' she said vehemently, her hands clenching on the stems of the cream and pale blue lisianthus, fragile and silky as poppies, in her bouquet. 'And we can prove it, thank heavens.'

'Don't worry about it; we'll deal with it.'

When he spoke like that, with such tough, unfaltering confidence, it was impossible not to believe that Drake could overcome anything. Olivia exhaled sharply. 'So what do we do now?'

'We play happy families, my brand-new wife, so persuasively that even the most hard-nosed family court judge will be convinced S—our son is in the best place.'

She nodded. 'And if the worst comes to the worst, we'll force my stepfather to take a DNA test. That must convince any judge not to give Simon to him, even if he is registered as his father.'

The car swung into the gateway. Olivia took comfort from the serene house, the timeless beauty of the trees and the garden. The news that her stepfather had made his move somehow steadied her. She had been terrified that he would try to kidnap Simon and carry him off— do, in fact, exactly what she had done. Now that she knew he was going the legal way about it, she was no longer afraid.

Or not quite so much. The thought of Simon left to Brian Harley's tender mercies filled her with horror, but Drake's emphatic profile reassured her. He wouldn't let that happen to his son.

'Try to forget what happened seven years ago; it's past and gone.' He sounded impatient, as though he thought she was foolish for continuing to worry.

'That's easy enough to *say*,' she said curtly, pitching her voice so that Simon couldn't hear. 'We've just got married because of what happened seven years ago. Can anyone simply ignore the past? Can you?'

His smile was ironic. 'I try,' he said obliquely. 'If you try, you can do anything.'

Sheer, relentless willpower probably could banish the effects of the past. Unfortunately it wasn't so easy for most people. Her past was too concrete, had overshadowed her life with its dark threat for far too long to be so swiftly dismissed.

A photographer waited for them, an angular woman in black with a scarlet beret perched on her orange hair, who had endless patience and a fund for anecdotes that eased the tension while she posed them and clicked.

This might be a mirror marriage—picture-perfect but insubstantial, a two-dimensional reflection of the real thing—yet Drake was going to a lot of trouble to make it seem genuine. Of course, his son's welfare depended on it.

And that was important to the man who was now her husband.

Over the days she'd been living in Drake's house she had grown to realise that whatever his reasons for not contacting his son before, he was now determined to be a good father.

Although there were only six at the wedding breakfast, it became a small celebration. Aura and Flint knew how to deal with an over-excited boy, and they both treated Phillips as an old friend. The champagne was vintage and the meal superb, and when Flint proposed a toast to the bride and groom in a witty, short speech, Olivia managed to look adoringly at Drake—a look he returned with an enigmatic little smile that fluttered her heart before he gave a short, succinct and just as entertaining reply.

Careful. The warning echoed through her mind. Fluttering hearts and this keen, lancing awareness were not on the agenda.

However, she decided when the Jensens had gone and the sky in the west was turning marigold over the Waitakere Ranges, Auckland's protection from the wild moods of the Tasman Sea, the day had gone rather well. Simon's future was a lot more secure now that they were married, and that was the main thing.

That had to be the main thing.

Regrettably, she wasn't so certain any more. Assailed by the uncomfortable feeling that she had delivered herself into Drake's hands, she suspected that keeping her heart free was not going to be easy. Simon's happiness might exact so high a price that she'd never be the same person again—but it was a price she was prepared to pay.

After hanging her dress in the wardrobe she creamed the cosmetics from her face, staring objectively at her reflection. Drake was right, damn his shrewd, discerning eye; she had the kind of healthy, unsubtle looks that would fade as quickly as her youth did. Even protected and cherished, fine, delicate skin like hers didn't wear well in New Zealand's harsh sun, and her honey-blonde hair would darken into anonymity.

Her mother had stayed radiantly beautiful until the day she died, and Drake's strong bone structure would ensure that he made a strikingly compelling old man, but she was the inconspicuous type who faded into the background.

Medium, she thought despairingly.

Medium in everything—looks, intelligence, height, personality. Not like Aura Jensen, who drew all eyes like the dark flame Drake had called her, nor like Elizabeth.

If she'd looked like either of those, Drake wouldn't have left her alone on their wedding night.

And that was why she was depressed.

She wanted him. And she had hoped that he wanted her enough to come to her. Worse than that, in spite of everything, she had to accept that the emotion she'd been trying so desperately to ignore was not simple desire, but an infinitely more complex thing. Love.

How stupid could she be?

Because although he might find her attractive, he wasn't in love with her. Oh, if she wanted it, there could be passion and commitment of a sort in their relationship, but she doubted whether he'd want children, or the sort of marriage she longed for.

Sighing, she turned away from the mirror. It was useless to worry. When Simon's happiness and well-being were certain, perhaps she could begin to make plans for this marriage she had engineered.

But nothing, she knew, as she pulled back the bed-clothes and crawled into the big, empty bed, nothing was going to assuage the consuming, white-hot need that ached through every cell in her body.

CHAPTER EIGHT

LOOKING up from the breakfast table, Drake said, 'You and I are seeing my solicitor this morning.'

Ever-present dread coagulated instantly in Olivia's stomach. She glanced at the door into the kitchen. From behind it came Simon's voice, clear and cheerful as he 'helped' Phillips make toast. A plan that had formed amorphously in her mind during the long sleepless night suddenly solidified.

'What,' Drake demanded in a vastly different voice, 'does that look mean?'

'If the decision goes against us—though I don't see how it can—I'll get Simon away, where my stepfather can't find us.'

'You will not.'

Her eyes searched his hard face as she said unevenly, 'Drake, you don't understand. If Simon is in danger—'

'I understand perfectly well,' he interrupted, a scathing note emphasising the words. 'Your only reaction to any sort of threat is to run away. Surely your own experience must have taught you that running away solves nothing. You have to stand and face threats, use your brains and your courage to overcome them, not turn and flee.'

'I've run away *once* in my life!'

'And you're planning to do it again,' he pointed out unanswerably. 'It's a pattern of behaviour you seem to be stuck in. I remember the flirtatious child-woman who spent an entire summer trying to persuade me into advancing, only to back off when things got too hot.'

'A good thing, surely?' She damped down the bitterness in her tone, adding in as bored a tone as she could muster, 'You might have made both my mother *and* me pregnant.'

His expression darkened, but Simon's laughter held back his reply.

Just as well, she thought, skin tightening over her flesh at the warning in his hooded eyes. His wordless response was every bit as antagonistic as her own feeling whenever she thought of him making love to her mother. With relief, she looked across to the door as Simon, proudly bearing a tray with toast on it, came into the room.

Drake drove her and Simon to the school, and went in with her to register him. He seemed to be enjoying the official part of parenthood. Effortlessly he charmed the headmistress and the infant teacher, as well as the class of embryo students, and impressed on the headmistress the fact that Simon was to be watched and never let out of the school grounds by himself.

'Custody problems?' the woman murmured.

'I'm afraid so,' Olivia said quietly.

'Don't worry about it. We have methods of dealing with this sort of distressing situation. He'll be picked up from school, I gather?'

'Every day,' Drake told her.

Hiding whatever curiosity she felt, the headmistress smiled at them both with a kind of sympathetic resignation. 'I'm sure he'll settle down well here.'

Simon had no doubts about that. They left him telling the class about playing cricket on the lawn. He didn't even notice them going.

'The solicitor first,' Drake said. 'Then I'll take you out to lunch.'

'You don't need to do that.'

'I think I might,' he murmured enigmatically.

There was nothing to be read in his face, and as they were in the press of traffic Olivia refrained from asking him what he meant.

By the time they walked out of the solicitor's office, however, she understood. Her guess that their marriage gave them the best chance of retaining custody of Simon had been reinforced, but the solicitor had impressed upon them both that they needed to be seen as a normal, happily married couple.

'And even then,' he said, 'I think you must accept the possibility that the registered father might be given access.'

'No!' Olivia couldn't hold back the word.

'Why not?' The solicitor frowned, shrewd eyes scanning her agitated face. 'The judge is going to take into consideration the fact that Brian Harley believes the child to be his own flesh and blood.'

Olivia glanced at Drake. How much had he told the man? As usual it was impossible to read anything in the hard face, although she was chilled by the studied detachment of his expression.

'He knows the child is not his,' Drake said. 'The child's mother—who was Olivia's mother—told him so before the child was born.'

'That, I'm afraid, is only your wife's word against his. Don't forget, he registered the boy as his child. Even if he did know the facts of Simon's parentage, he clearly intended to treat him as his own. However, the fact that he now knows he's not might alter our response if he suggests access. It was unfortunate, Mrs Arundell, that you decided to run away with the boy. It gives your stepfather moral standing—especially if he can prove that he tried to find you both.'

Olivia flushed at the implied criticism. 'I had good reasons.'

'It would help if we knew what they were.'

Colour drained from her skin. A cold sweat sprang out at her temples and across her upper lip. She said huskily, 'I—'

'Is it of vital importance?' Drake interposed.

'If it's going to show Brian Harley as an unfit father, then, yes, I'd say it was important.' The solicitor was pleasant but inexorable.

'I can't prove anything,' Olivia said in a low voice, staring at the floor. 'As you said before, it would just be my word against his.'

'We'll discuss it later,' Drake said, with more than a hint of steely authority in the words.

'Yes, of course. Try not to worry, Mrs Arundell. On the face of it we seem to have a pretty good case,' the solicitor said reassuringly.

Drake took her to lunch at one of the city's elegant restaurants, where Olivia did her best to look as confident and composed as he did. She had been to restaurants before, of course, but it had been five years since she had eaten out, and never in such a casually sophisticated place. Even in her new clothes she felt slightly dowdy. The pale aqua linen had seemed very smart when she chose it, but in this place she looked almost countryish amongst the elegantly dressed women.

Some, she thought critically, overdressed. Surely one didn't don silk, however cobwebby, for lunch on a warm, early winter day?

'Smile.'

The curt command fell unpleasantly on her ears. However, she pinned on what she hoped would appear to be a spontaneous smile as she asked, 'Why?'

'You heard John O'Sullivan. We have to project an image of happiness,' he said. 'Do you know anyone in Auckland?'

'A few people.' Afraid that making friends might lead to discovery, she had kept very much to herself at the flat. 'Why?'

'We need to be seen by as many influential people as possible—preferably people who'll be prepared to stand up in court and swear to our compatibility and obvious commitment to each other. *Smile!*'

Obeying the forceful instruction, issued through lips that were curved in a way that managed to be commanding and profoundly exciting at the same time, she drew in a deep breath, leaned towards him, and beamed, letting her eyes cling to his.

'Good girl,' he said, taking her hand with a dazzling, experienced, sexy smile that set her pulse-rate soaring through the stratosphere.

She was sure that every conversation in the restaurant died away. The clutch of response in her stomach tightened unbearably; the effects of his smile slid from nerve-end to nerve-end all the way down to the soles of her feet, curling her toes in sheer, shivering reaction.

'That,' he said, his eyes shimmering as clear and translucent as the best pale jade, 'is more like it.'

He released her hand and looked up. Materialising by magic, a waiter asked them what they would like to drink.

Within minutes they were sipping a wine with a fresh, invigorating flavour, mellowed by the faintest hint of... 'Passion fruit?' she questioned. 'Surely it's not a fruit wine?'

'No, it's a Marlborough Sauvignon Blanc. Do you like it?'

She nodded. 'Very much.'

His lifted brows made her feel shy, but he said, 'Good. It's a favourite of mine,' and finished giving their orders.

He entertained her by relaying the exploits of his Hawaiian business contact who, deciding that New Zealand was the last frontier, had put himself through such ordeals as black-water rafting, cycling through the Haast Pass and tramping some of the more difficult tracks in the South Island high country, finishing his tour of that island by bungee jumping from a bridge in the Kawerau Gorge near Queenstown.

Because he had a dry wit, and his affection and respect for the man were obvious, Olivia enjoyed his story immensely. Her laughter, however, was cut off by a low, seductive voice.

'Darling,' it murmured as the vision who owned it bent to kiss Drake on the cheek, 'how wonderful to see you here. I thought you ate your lunch from a brown paper bag at your desk. We'll make a civilised person of you yet!'

A complex combination of emotions seared through Olivia—jealousy, a savage pain and despair such as she had never known before, and an unnerving possessiveness that made her want to drag the lovely stranger away from Drake and tell her in very forceful terms that he was not her darling any longer.

Of course Drake's response gave nothing away. Smiling a little teasingly, he got to his feet. 'Hello, Jan,' he said. 'How are you?'

'Fine.' Slightly slanted eyes the deep, intense blue of a midwinter sky surveyed him thoroughly, before flicking with devastating—and well-practised—suddenness to Olivia's face. 'Aren't you going to introduce us?'

Her tone conveyed nothing more than polite curiosity, yet Olivia stiffened.

'This is my wife,' Drake said smoothly. 'Olivia, this is Jan Carruthers, an old friend.'

'How do you do?' Olivia held out her hand.

Although Jan shook it automatically, her surprise was transparent. 'Wife! That was sudden, surely?'

Something disturbing gleamed in Drake's eyes. 'I fell in love with Olivia when she was seventeen,' he said, adding with a smile that was a masterly combination of tenderness and intensity as he looked at Olivia, 'but I had to go off to make my fortune. We were married yesterday.'

By now Jan Carruthers had rallied. Dropping Olivia's hand, she said, 'Felicitations, my dear.' Her smile narrowed. Turning her head to give Olivia an excellent view of her perfect profile, she said to Drake, 'And I must congratulate you, of course. I must say, you've kept it very quiet!'

'There's a notice in the paper today,' he said, startling Olivia.

'Well, you could have given some of your old friends a hint.' An admonitory finger lingered along his cheekbone, prompting another stab of jealousy that gritted Olivia's teeth.

Smiling at Drake from beneath lashes that were long and thick and real, the newcomer went on, 'How the mighty are fallen! We'd have loved to come along and see the impregnable Drake Arundell leg-roped and bailed. My dear, I must tell you—' she turned to Olivia and dropped her pretty voice confidentially '—that women fall over themselves in droves—'

'Careful, Jan, your dairy-farming roots are showing,' Drake interposed, with a smile that didn't quite reach his eyes and a note in his voice that hinted at warning.

Someone, Olivia thought acidly, was going to get drowned in those undercurrents, but it wasn't going to be her.

'I come from a long line of doctors,' Jan said, dropping the worldly sophistication for a delighted gurgle of laughter that made Olivia wonder if she had read the situation incorrectly. This Jan Carruthers could become a friend. 'As you well know, you beast. Listen, why don't you come to a party I'm giving on Saturday night so you can introduce Olivia to everyone?'

'I'm sorry,' Drake said without hesitation, 'we're already booked up that night.'

It wasn't exactly a snub—he spoke in a perfectly pleasant tone—but Jan sent Olivia a swift, startled look as though she blamed her for his response.

'Some other time, then,' she said, recovering her poise enough to bestow a glorious smile on them both. 'I'll ring you, Olivia, and organise it.' Her gaze flicked past Olivia and she said quickly, 'I must go. Goodbye.'

Clearly she was almost desperate to get away, but she had left her move too late. From behind Olivia another female voice said, 'Hello, I didn't realise we were meeting you, Drake.'

Jan Carruthers said, 'We aren't.' Astonishingly, her glance met Olivia's with something like a fierce instruction in their depths. 'This is my sister,' she said. 'Anet, this is Olivia, who has just married Drake.'

The newcomer was an Amazon, over six feet tall, broad-shouldered and powerfully built. For one horrified second Olivia saw anguish haunt eyes the pure translucent silver of moonlight—beautiful eyes set in a striking face. At once she understood Jan's wordless command. All she could do for Anet was give her time to cope with her emotions.

'Hello,' she said, smiling. 'How lovely to meet you.' Holding out her hand, she went on cheerfully, 'I realise this must be an awful shock to Drake's friends, but it isn't as sudden as it seems. We've known each other for years—in fact, we grew up together in the same little town in Hawke's Bay.'

Her hand was almost enveloped by a large, long-fingered one, very strong.

The consuming despair had been wiped from Anet Carruthers' expression as though it had never existed. In a deep, musical voice, she said, 'I hope you'll both be very happy.'

She turned and held out her hand to Drake. Nothing but affection showed in the hard grey-green eyes as he shook hands. 'Thank you, Anet,' he said. 'How's the physiotherapy coming on?'

'I'm getting there.' Her smile was steady.

If her glance clung a moment too long to his face Olivia didn't mind. For this woman she felt nothing but compassion, because she knew how she'd feel if Drake told her he had married another woman.

'We'd better go.' Jan almost bristled with a blatant protectiveness that reminded Olivia of a terrier attempting to protect a Rottweiler. 'We don't want to be late, Anet.'

'You're right,' Anet said, smiling down at her sister. 'Nice to have met you, Olivia.'

Olivia waited until they had taken their table on the other side of the room before asking quietly, 'Should you be telling me something about Anet?'

Anyone but Drake would have been taken aback by her bluntness, but he merely lifted saturnine brows. 'You'll hear a lot,' he said casually, although his eyes were very keen, 'most of it rubbish.'

She sipped some more of the wine, her mouth curling against the cool rim of the glass. 'I liked her.'

'Everyone does. She has never been my lover. Nor have I given her any reason to believe that I would like her to be.' He spoke with crisp austerity.

'It's all right,' Olivia said drily. 'If we'd had a whirlwind romance I might find her threatening, but as it is, it doesn't matter.'

Some disconcerting light flashed into the depths of his eyes, vanishing as he reasserted that ironclad control over his emotions. 'You are, of course, perfectly correct,' he said with bland courtesy, putting her in her place.

Heat singed her cheekbones, then ebbed, leaving her oddly desolate. Fortunately the waiter arrived with their food, and the sticky moment was lost in the discreet bustle.

It was a splendid meal. Mainly they talked about Simon—Olivia filling his father in on the past years, trying to give him some idea of the personality of his son. At last, however, Drake looked up, and their waiter came back and did whatever waiters do, so that within a few minutes Olivia was floating out of the restaurant, her hand tucked confidingly in the crook of Drake's arm.

She knew what was happening to her. This was what it had been like when she was seventeen; she had floated then too, lost in a fool's dream of love. Although they'd never exchanged anything but words and smouldering looks and that one kiss, that first love had been very real to her. And it had been betrayed cruelly by the two people she'd loved the most.

Had they known? Drake almost certainly had; he'd targeted her, used her to hide his illicit liaison with her mother.

She was not going to set herself up for that again. But just for this afternoon, the day after her wedding, she would pretend a little...

She was brought abruptly down to earth. 'I have to go to the office,' he said as they reached the street. 'I'm sorry, but I have a business meeting set up that I can't avoid. I shouldn't be too late home.'

It was stupid to be so shattered. 'That's fine,' she said airily. She should be grateful to him for showing her once again how foolish it was to fantasise.

He looked at her with hooded eyes, his mouth compressed. 'I'm sorry, it's not much of a start for a marriage. And I can't promise that it's going to be much better soon; I'm going to be busy for another couple of months. In August we'll take a proper holiday. Decide where you'd rather go—to the tropics, or on a skiing holiday.'

And, perhaps to make sure she didn't get the wrong idea, he added, 'Skiing might be best, as Simon isn't allowed to swim with those grommets in his ears, is he?'

'No,' she said, smiling inanely. 'He'd love to ski, I'm sure.'

He put her in a taxi and she went home through a golden afternoon to find Phillips ironing clothes in the kitchen.

Perhaps emboldened by the wine, she said, 'We are going to have to find me something to do, otherwise I'll die of boredom.'

He continued ironing a large teatowel. 'I see. What do you like doing?'

'Flowers,' she said succinctly. 'I am very good at arranging flowers. And making pickles. I like gardening too.'

'A man comes three times a week to do the garden.'

'That's fine, but I'd like to feel that some part of it is mine. I'll have a talk to him. What do you dislike doing?'

He gave her a wry look from beneath his permanently surprised brows. 'Flowers. And I don't set tables very well. But you'll have to check it with Drake.'

Unable to budge him from that, she left him, wondering rather forlornly what she could find to do with herself all day in this huge, empty house. Arranging flowers and setting tables was not going to take up much of each day. How on earth was she going to fill up the ten months before the next university year began?

She was standing on the terrace looking out across the sparkling waters of the bay, a frown pleating her brows, when Phillips emerged from inside the house.

'I'm just going to get Simon,' he said. 'Would you like to come?'

She nodded. Life had suddenly fallen flat. For years she had been too exhausted to have time to think, so caught up in the hard realities of stretching an inadequate amount of money to cover living expenses that she simply hadn't had time to plan.

Now it was all over. Drake had taken everything into his capable hands, and she felt as useful as a wetsuit in a desert.

Apart from her stepfather's claim to custody Simon was safe, his future protected. Others were taking their places in his affections; he was clearly overwhelmed by Drake, already edging towards a whole-hearted adoration, and he thought Phillips was a splendid person. Both names were appearing more and more frequently in his conversation.

She wasn't jealous, she told herself. Just—a little sad.

And lost. The one constant love in her life wasn't going to be taken from her, but Simon's affection no longer fulfilled her emotional needs.

She wanted the man who had had an affair with her mother, got her pregnant and abandoned her cruelly.

Worse than that. It wasn't enough to be the object of Drake's intense masculine sexuality; she passionately yearned for him to love her.

It was, she finally admitted, the reason she had asked him to marry her. Oh, she'd wanted to safeguard Simon, but if she hadn't been in love with Drake she'd have found some other way.

There was nothing to be done about it. It was agonising to be so humiliatingly, helplessly in thrall to him, but her heart didn't seem able to take any cognisance of common sense and practicalities. She had followed him into this mirror world and been captured all over again, so she'd just have to deal with it as well as she could. With a small, ironic smile pinned to her mouth, she got her bag and went out to the car with Phillips.

Simon had had a magnificent day, and kept them entertained with details from it until he finally went to bed. It was then that he said, 'I could hear everything, Liv. The teacher sat me up the front, but she didn't need to 'cause I could hear just like all the other kids.'

It was worth it, she thought, hugging him close. Any sacrifice, even that of her heart, was worth it for Simon.

Downstairs, Drake was working in the office, but he came to the door as she went past and asked, 'Is he asleep yet?'

'No,' she said. 'He's waiting for you to go up.'

'What's the matter?'

She tried a smile. 'Oh, nothing. It's just that—he can hear. I haven't thanked you, but I—I—'

His arm about her shoulders silenced the trembling words as she fought for control. 'You'd do anything for Simon, wouldn't you?' he said quietly.

She nodded. 'For most of his life there's only been me, you see, to care for him.'

'Well, he has a father now.'

'I know.' She tried to drag her mind away from the far too weakening comfort of strong arms and the steady beat of his heart against her cheek, the elusive, almost subliminally experienced scent of male, clean and musky, that sent pulses of sensation racing through her body. At last she said gruffly, 'He needs a father.'

'It's hard to give up responsibility,' he said, surprising her with his astuteness. 'But although he still needs you more than he needs me, we're his family now. I know we went into this for practical reasons, but I can't see why we shouldn't make a great success of this marriage, Olivia, if we work at it.'

Half dazed by her overpowering response to his closeness, she nodded. She could, she thought dreamily, stay like this for the rest of her life...

'I'll go up and say goodnight to him,' Drake said, putting her to one side.

Dashed, Olivia went into the sitting room. When Drake came back she was ostensibly reading a magazine. She looked up, willing herself to look merely enquiring, not as though she had glimpsed the border of paradise and had it rudely torn away.

'He's decided he's going to be a dustman when he grows up. Apparently he was most impressed by the truck this morning.'

Olivia laughed. 'That's about the fifth vocation he's discovered, and all of them have involved dirt in some form or another. Typical for a boy of six.'

'Very. I had great ambitions to be a grader driver. Do you mind if I watch television?' he asked. 'There's a documentary on the peoples of the Pacific Rim that's supposed to be excellent.'

It was, but although she enjoyed it, Olivia enjoyed even more sitting beside him on the wide, comfortable sofa, her peripheral vision filled with his presence, big and lean and unsettling as he watched the television screen. By turning her head very slightly she could see his profile, hard-edged and resolute, the straight nose and determined jaw proclaiming his character to anyone who cared to look behind the shattering masculine magnetism.

The physical need that ached through her whenever she was near him stirred again—a slow, acute pleasure that was almost pain. Like pearls on a string, she slid his words through her mind: 'I can't see why we shouldn't make a great success of this marriage, Olivia, if we work at it.'

Was that a subtle way of saying that he hoped their marriage might one day become real?

Her heart leapt in her throat, and the television reporter's words became a muted accompaniment to her dreams. For a moment the future spread before her, fair and full of promise, as familiar yet unknown as a landscape seen in a mirror. Could she turn the good, sensible marriage he thought they should be able to achieve, the haven where Simon would be safe and happy, into the sort of union her heart craved, where contentment and passion would be irradiated by love?

Oh, yes—if only Drake were not the man who had seduced and betrayed her mother.

Nothing—not the desire he roused in her, not the love for him that had struggled so shamefully into flower—could overcome that fact.

For seven years that knowledge had been burned into her brain, yet even now, after she had practically had to force him to accept his responsibilities, she was still trying to find some good reason for his behaviour.

But the only thing that could excuse it would be if he hadn't known of Simon's existence.

Basically it came down to deciding which of them, Drake or her mother, had lied. Because one of them certainly had.

Why should Elizabeth have lied?

There was no reason, whereas there was a very good reason for Drake to twist the truth; it made him look better in her eyes. If you wanted a normal marriage then a lie that would absolve you of some of the blame might be a small price to pay.

Oh, he had powerful allies—the fifth column in her heart. Desire was notorious for scrambling one's thoughts, for making fools of the most sensible women.

More than anything she wanted to make love with him, to give him whatever he wanted from her, to take whatever she could from him. She wanted him so much that she couldn't sleep at night because her body was on fire for him.

From somewhere in her mind there emerged the face of the woman in the miniature. Surprisingly dark brows had drawn together in a frown, and the full, pretty lips were clamped in a straight line.

Get out of my mind, damn you!

The ribbons and feathers flounced as the unknown woman gave a very firm shake of her head and a stern, admonitory glare.

Olivia yawned. She must have fallen asleep for just a second.

'Tired?' Drake's voice was cool, almost amused. Looping an arm around her shoulders he pulled her against him. 'It'll be finished soon.'

It was seductively easy to lean her cheek on the hard width of his chest, to watch the screen with eyes that merely registered colour and movement, to hear the reporter's voice with ears that were attuned only to the solid, heavy thump of Drake's heart.

Get up and run all the way to your bedroom! her mind commanded, but when his arm contracted and one hand came to rest on her ribs, just below her breast, her blood filled with bubbles that exploded to release a dazzling joy.

The curved trunks of coconut palms framing a turquoise lagoon wavered on the screen as the professionally interested tones of the reporter faded into a soft theme tune. A small click silenced the set, and then Drake turned her into his arms and looked at her, his eyes intent and measuring, the silver gleam in the green very pronounced.

'You look sleepy and delicious,' he murmured, and kissed her waiting mouth.

Her whole being sang in delight, in wonder at the splendid shock of his mouth, his scent in her nostrils, the coiled power that spoke subliminally to all that was female in her. Although in the distant reaches of her brain some despairing remnant of common sense warned her that she was going to regret this, she didn't move.

How could she regret this magnificent passion, so completely without calculation, so potently primeval? This was what she had been born for. Everything about her was transformed by his touch, by his mouth and his caress, her body brought to life for the first time, quickened by his consuming sensuality.

'Open your mouth,' he ordered against her lips. 'Yes, like that...'

She knew about such kisses, of course; she might be inexperienced and out of touch, but she wasn't naïve. What she hadn't suspected was their effect on her. At the first invasion of his tongue her whole body stiffened and wildfire flared though her, collecting in a conflagration in the pit of her stomach, a conflagration that burned out of control, turning to ashes everything but the increasing desperation of desire.

Without volition she arched in a vain effort to satisfy its demands. Drake laughed beneath his breath and kissed the long line of her throat—small, biting kisses that fanned the flames. Her breasts felt full and tender, and the craving that had kept her awake these past nights pierced every cell inside her.

'Tell me what you want,' he said, his voice deep and smoky and indolent. 'I don't know how I've managed to keep my hands off you—tell me that you've wanted me too, that you've lain awake at night aching with need, with desire...'

Shivering, she whispered, 'Oh, yes. For eternity...'

With a strength that awed her, he lifted her across the muscles that flexed then contracted in his thighs. For the first time in her life Olivia was overwhelmed by longing, a hunger so basic and primeval that it was like a force of nature.

Weighted by passion, her lashes fell. Without speaking, she watched his hands, their colour a shocking contrast to the pale material of her shirt, flick free the buttons. Her stomach tensed; eager and expectant, athrill with new sensations, clamouring for the one, the inevitable ending, she lay with parted lips and slumbrous eyes.

'I want it to be perfect for you,' he said thickly, freeing the clasp of her bra. He pulled the straps down over her arms and looked at the soft curves of ivory skin that his caresses were warming with a translucent tint.

The intangible heat of his regard scorched across her skin. Her breasts seemed to tighten, and an incredible feeling flowed from the peaking areolae. He bent his head so that the devil-sparks in his hair dazzled her with fire snared in ebony. When he spoke, the words danced like imps on her sensitised skin.

'You're beautiful,' he said in a low, rough voice. 'I want to pleasure you so much that you become addicted to me, just as I'm becoming addicted to you...'

The words died as his mouth closed around a pointed, receptive tip. Her body bucked as an exquisite pang flashed through her, melting her, drowning her, sweet as honey, savage and feral as fire, will-sapping as alcohol. Heat suffused her skin; she heard the little groans that forced themselves up from her throat but couldn't stop them, just as she couldn't stop her instinctive clutch at him.

'Yes,' he said. 'I need to feel your hands on me, Olivia. Touch me...'

It was like being given the key to treasure beyond price. The tips of her fingers tingled as she delicately traced the hard swell of muscle, discovered the smoothness of his skin, toyed with the fine covering of hair. Slowly she lifted a shadowed, drowsy gaze to his face.

Her heart missed a beat. The skin seemed to have tightened over the arrogant bones, so that he reminded her of a predator, intent upon one thing only—subjugation. For the first time she realised just where this was heading—surrender, not only of her body, scary enough in itself, but of her heart and her life. If she let this continue she was going to yield every part of herself to the man who had slept with her mother.

Something of her sudden, horrified panic must have shown in her face, because he froze, astonishment and fury mingling in the grey-green eyes.

'Olivia,' he said, the straight, worldly mouth oddly tense, 'I'm not going to hurt you, I swear. Don't look at me like that...'

A harsh, shuddering breath shook her.

'All right. Get off me.' And when she didn't move immediately his voice cracked out, 'Now, damn you!'

The rigid tension of his body communicated its own warning; with undignified haste she scrambled from his lap, pulling her clothes together with trembling hands, her brain fighting to recover some mastery of her unwilling, turbulent body.

'So you're still the little tease who had every male under thirty in Springs Flat going around with a permanent erection,' he said unforgivably, watching her efforts with glittering eyes.

A discreet knock on the door brought him to his feet. He ran a hand through the dark hair, swore a succinct and startling oath, and said, 'Yes, what is it?'

Phillips pushed the door open and said tonelessly, 'There's a Mr Brian Harley at the door.' He paused, then added, 'He has a young lady with him. He says she is a nanny.'

Olivia's gasp hung like a small explosion in the air. Some unspoken communication crackled between Drake and Phillips, before Drake transferred his gaze to Olivia. She could read nothing in his expression, no emotion in the chilly grey-green eyes. Nothing.

'All right,' he said. 'Bring him in here. She can wait in the hall. Keep an eye on her.'

Her stepfather walked in with the calm air of one who had no reason to suspect failure. After one quick look Olivia kept her eyes rigidly away from him, but that complacent self-possession sent warning bells jangling.

'What do you want?' Drake asked without preamble.

Brian Harley's smile was superior and gratingly assured. 'I've come for my son,' he said.

'He is *not* your son,' Olivia flashed. 'He's Drake's son, as you well know.'

Her stepfather looked from her white, vehement face to that of the man who stood beside her.

'So you haven't told her,' he said significantly, his eyes cynically amused. 'Go on, Arundell. Tell her what the DNA test showed.'

Olivia transferred her gaze from Drake's impassive face to that of her stepfather, lit by the gloating satisfaction that still had the power to terrify her.

'Or shall I?' he sneered.

Drake directed an indifferent glance at him, then turned to meet Olivia's eyes. 'I can't prove that Simon is my son,' he said.

Searching his face for signs that this was a terrible joke, she gasped, 'What do you mean—you can't prove it?' She stared at him as though he'd turned crazy. 'You had the DNA test—you told me—'

'He lied,' Brian Harley said with relish. 'Because the boy isn't his son.'

'But the test—'

The older man lost patience. 'Drake Arundell is just as big a liar as your slut of a mother. The DNA test proves conclusively that he's no relation to the boy. At least he's got some common sense; he knows it's stupid to proceed with a court case he can't win, which is why he agreed to let his lawyer release the information to mine.'

Olivia looked at Drake, mutely asking for reassurance, but could read nothing in his impassive countenance. Every muscle in her body clenched with fear. 'Drake?' she whispered.

'It's true.' He didn't even look at the man who stood so triumphantly opposite them. Drake's eyes, cold and piercing as lances, were fixed on her face.

She couldn't believe it, but paradoxically, because it was Drake who said so, she had to. 'But—why did you lie to me?'

Her stepfather said, 'Revenge, you fool. Everything he's done has been motivated by his need for revenge against me. Though if Elizabeth hadn't told me that he was the father of her child I wouldn't have—'

'Sacked my father? Embezzled my money?' Drake supplied with chilling precision.

Shakily Olivia spread her fingers across the back of her head, pressing hard as she stared at the two antagonists. It was slowly being borne in on her that she and Simon were merely pawns in a battle that had started all those years ago.

How *stupid* she had been.

Brian Harley blustered, 'I wouldn't have done it if she hadn't lied. Damn it, I stood up for you when your father wanted you to go to university and all you wanted to do was race cars! Didn't I? I persuaded him to let you have your chance!'

Drake showed his teeth. 'So I, like a fool, sent all my winnings back to you to invest. And you systematically, cleverly and carefully lost them.'

'It was because she lied,' Brian Harley said, almost pleadingly. 'You must understand—you stabbed me in the back. You slept with her.'

'But I didn't,' Drake said silkily. 'Incidentally, how did you find that out?'

'Remember when you came to Springs Flat to find out what the hell I'd done with your money? I told you and you clenched your fist and asked me why. That's all you said—"Why?" And I laughed and told you I knew you were Elizabeth's lover. Oh, you hid your shock damned fast, but I saw the astonishment in your face, and the disbelief. It was then I realised the bitch had lied to me. So I've known all along that you had no claim to the boy. And you've married Olivia for nothing.'

He glanced at Olivia's appalled expression and said, 'Perhaps you'll believe me now, you stupid little fool, when I tell you he's not interested in you or the kid; he wants to get even with me.'

Drake said calmly, 'Get out.'

But Brian Harley managed to claw back his disintegrating composure. 'Look, let's deal,' he said quickly. 'You hand the boy over to me and I won't prosecute her for kidnapping him in the first place. Otherwise I'm going to the police tomorrow.'

'I wouldn't hand a dog over to you,' Olivia spat. 'And if you prosecute me for kidnapping I'll tell them what I know about my mother's death.'

He stared at her. 'What the hell are you talking about?'

'I know you killed her,' she said baldly.

He narrowed his eyes. 'You're mad,' he said, the satisfaction in his tone rudely shaking her entrenched convictions. 'Good. That will make it much easier for me. No court will give custody to a madwoman—especially when she's in prison for kidnapping.'

Switching his attention to Drake, he demanded, 'Well, do we have a deal or not? I'm not going to hurt the kid—he'll be looked after far better than she's ever been able to—and if you hand him over now she'll stay out of prison.'

'No, we don't have a deal.' Drake's voice was even and emotionless.

With no signal that Olivia could discern, the door opened and Phillips stood there.

'All right, I'll go, but you'll be hearing from me again,' Brian Harley said, his voice unpleasant with anticipation. 'The boy is registered as my son, and you have no claim on him at all.'

Silently Olivia waited until the muted thud of the front door indicated that Phillips had shown him out, then turned and blundered across the floor.

'Where are you going?'

'Up to my room.' The words came slowly, thickly, past a throat taut with fear and disillusion.

He said, 'Don't you want to hear any more?'

She shook her head quickly. There was an expanding emptiness where her heart used to be, and she felt sick and cold and beaten. 'No. You've got your revenge,' she said. 'You don't need me to help you enjoy it.'

He waited until she got to the door before saying in a voice that chilled her to the heart, 'Don't, not for a moment, think of leaving me, Olivia. Your days of running away are over. We are married, and we stay married.'

'Even if I never trust you again?'

His voice revealed that he was approaching her. 'You've never trusted me, Olivia. You even made me write out a receipt for that bloody miniature. Fortunately, trust isn't particularly important when we have this.'

His hand was cruel on her shoulder as he turned her around. Bending, he kissed her white lips with insulting expertise, holding her relentlessly against his body until the sheer male energy got through to her and she was betrayed by her own needs, her own weakness.

When he lifted his head there was a ruthless satisfaction in the depths of his eyes. He ran a slow, insulting hand from the soft, throbbing hollow in her throat down over the thrusting peak of her breast. 'Fight it as hard as you can,' he said, 'but you belong to me, body and soul. You can't escape me—just as I can't escape you.'

This time he made no attempt to detain her when she walked from the room.

In her bedroom she sank down in front of the mirror and looked at her reflection—eyes dimmed to a cloudy brown by shock and pain, a drawn face left sallow by a total lack of colour.

Simple lust was no reason for marriage; she couldn't believe that he wanted her so much he had been prepared to marry her. Drake was too controlled, too self-sufficient to relinquish his freedom and surrender to an overwhelming passion.

Which left revenge as his only possible motivation.

And that she could believe only too well.

Now, she thought bleakly, she knew why he had gone to work on the Pacific island where he'd met Phillips; no longer able to race, he'd been cheated of his winnings. To get himself into a position where he could strip Brian Harley of his assets he'd needed a financial base.

Yes, it had to be revenge. Brian Harley had ruthlessly sacked Drake's father, not caring in the least that Mrs Arundell had been so ill; no wonder Drake hated him enough to ignore such concepts as justice and mercy.

She bit her lip so fiercely that it almost bled. Oh God, what was going to happen to Simon?

Groping in her drawer for a handkerchief, her fingers closed on a crackle of paper. She drew it out. The receipt Drake had written for the miniature. Symbol of her lack of trust.

How very right she had been!

Well, she demanded of the woman in the miniature, what now? You've orchestrated this whole thing, now tell me what I'm supposed to do?

But although she could summon the woman's face to her mind's eye, there was no help there. It was just a portrait of great charm and psychological insight, nothing more; certainly it had none of the half-mystical powers Olivia had somehow fastened onto it.

Scrubbing her eyes with the handkerchief, she got to her feet. Exhaustion lay like lead in her bones; she'd had too many shocks to be able to think clearly. First she'd have a long shower and then she'd get the rest she so badly needed.

But when she came back into the bedroom she couldn't go to bed; her body might be tired, but queries chased themselves around her brain, scuppering any chance of sleep. She sat down on the side of the bed and stared down at her clasped hands.

Who was Simon's father? She could summon no one to mind. Elizabeth had stamped her impress on both her children to the exclusion of their fathers, so it was no use searching for a physical resemblance. Anyway, there had been no other man around that summer.

She tried to recall the events, ticking off the small-town parties and occasions, the barbecues and Christmas festivities, the picnics and dinners. Her mother and stepfather had had a circle of friends that hadn't changed much over the years, but there had been no one there that summer who could have seduced Elizabeth into an affair.

It had to have been someone local. Her mother had lied, which meant that she'd known her husband had the power to harm her lover. So he had to have been someone who'd lived close by, someone she'd needed to protect.

Who?

CHAPTER NINE

AFTER a troubled night of little sleep and much anguish, she woke to an aching head and slow tears burning behind her eyes, but she was not allowed the luxury of time to collect her thoughts or lick her wounds. A sharp knock on the door had her sitting upright, her hands clutching the sheet in panic.

'Who is it?' she croaked, eyes dilating as the door was pushed open.

Drake stood there, his brows drawn together in a frown. 'Get up,' he said succinctly. 'Your stepfather is here with his lawyer.'

'What?'

'You heard. Get up and come down to the office as fast as you can.'

Five minutes later, dressed in jeans and a light jersey, face washed, teeth cleaned and hair combed into some sort of order, she walked in through the door of the office, face set in lines of stony purpose. Whatever happened, she would keep Simon safe.

'Ah, Olivia, come in,' Drake said, rising to his feet. He held out his hand, and when she put hers into it drew her close and kissed her, then stood with her in the safe circle of his arms where only she could see the warning in the cold grey-green depths of his eyes.

'Where is Simon?' she demanded.

Drake put her into a chair beside the desk. 'He's with Phillips,' he said. 'Your stepfather's solicitor is waiting in the sitting room.'

She turned a smouldering glance onto Brian Harley's face. 'What do you want?'

He shrugged. 'We can do this easily,' he said, not attempting to hide his satisfaction, 'or we can do it hard. Either you hand the boy over to me now, or I go with my solicitor to the police station and swear that you kidnapped him five years ago. I doubt if any family court judge is going to award custody to a woman in prison for kidnapping. And as Arundell isn't any relation to the boy, and in the absence of any other claimant, custody will automatically be awarded to me.'

He was bluffing. He had to be. Yet there was a frightening confidence in his voice that sent cold shivers through Olivia. Oh God, she thought, sending a furious look at Drake, why hadn't she been a little more clever last night? She and Simon could have been well gone by now.

'Not necessarily,' Drake said smoothly. 'For several reasons: first of all, the court might be interested to know why you didn't tell the police five years ago that Olivia had stolen Simon from you. And a family court judge might be even more interested in the fact that Simon is the only grandson and heir of Simon Brentshaw, who left him several million dollars when he died.'

For the first time in her life Olivia saw Brian Harley at a loss.

His recovery was quick, however. He blustered, 'What the hell are you talking about? Brentshaw was obsessed with the belief that children who grow up rich go to the pack. His favourite proverb was from rags to rags in three generations. He left his money to charity. Everyone knows that.'

'I'm told he was rather tedious about it, but he must have decided that believing one had no money was just as good as actually having none, because he set up a secret trust for Simon just before he died.' Drake's voice was coolly relentless.

'He set one up for Olivia and her mother too, but it was much smaller, and as you were the sole trustee you were able to plunder it without anyone realising what had happened. That's why you went to Australia without making any effort to find Olivia and Simon, or even reporting them missing.

'I suppose you thought Olivia's trust would be enough for you. And if you'd lived sensibly it would have been. Unfortunately you got carried away and decided to make lots more money quickly, using hers as seed money. But the real estate deals went down, and now you've got creditors baying for your blood.'

Olivia felt like Phillips, her brows pinned into perpetual astonishment. Why hadn't Drake told her this last night?

Because he had been furious with her, she thought wearily. She had more or less accused him of using her to get revenge. Oh, God, what had she done?

Brian Harley blurted, 'You did it! You threatened to bring me down and you've—'

'Don't be a fool,' Drake said, his tone bored and dismissive. 'Yes, I was young enough and angry enough to make threats, but life is too short for revenge. Anyway, you didn't need help to bankrupt yourself—you did it quite easily on your own.'

Brian Harley got to his feet. 'You can't prove any of this,' he sneered. 'Oh, I'll admit that her trust is empty, but it was bad investments that did that, and there's no way you can prove otherwise.'

'Late last night a courier brought me some interesting documents, one of which is a run-down on the expenses you've claimed over the years—expenses which are outrageous. They make intriguing reading,' Drake said implacably. 'I'm sure the Fraud Office will find them as fascinating as I did.'

'This is preposterous,' Brian Harley shouted, his face scarlet and truculent. He thrust his head forward, glowering at Drake. 'Lies—nothing but lies.'

Drake's smile had all the warmth and empathy of a wolf as it makes the killing leap. 'You are broke, Harley. I've had people working hard these last few weeks, unravelling your affairs in Australia. They make very damning reading. Unless you can lay your hands on millions of dollars within the next couple of months you're going to end up bankrupt—which could be the least of your worries.

'And that brings us to Simon, and your sudden, unexpected desire to give him a home. If he's living with you, you'll be entitled to use money from the trust to support him. You need that money, otherwise your little empire in Australia will go under, and you with it. And then there'll be questions asked, and odds are you'll end up in prison for a long time.'

There was a moment's silence. Licking his lips, Brian Harley watched Drake with the fear and baffled fury of a cornered animal.

Drake resumed, 'Of course, all of this would sound rather mercenary in front of a family court judge.'

Her stepfather said angrily, 'The brat is illegitimate, anyway. He isn't entitled to it—not morally.'

'There is no such thing as an illegitimate child in New Zealand,' Drake said with biting contempt. 'And a man is entitled to leave his money to whoever he wants to.' He paused, before adding reflectively, 'And then, of course, there's the question of how Elizabeth died.'

Brian Harley's head came up. His gaze swung from the hard, implacable countenance of his enemy to Olivia's. Dangerously he stated, 'I had nothing to do with her death.'

'Tell him,' Drake ordered.

Olivia shivered, yet the compulsion in Drake's eyes forced the words from her. As she spoke she saw her stepfather's face set into stone.

When her words had died away in the quiet room he uttered a raw curse. 'All right, I went to her room and I hit her—but not hard enough to kill her.'

'Hard enough to make her dizzy,' Drake said ruthlessly, 'so that she tripped and hit her head.'

'Not while I was there,' Brian Harley said quickly. 'I didn't kill her. As for the boy—' He broke off, then said furiously, 'You had a bloody nerve, thinking I'd kill a child! I wouldn't have hurt him.'

Somehow, she believed him.

Over the years he had assumed monstrous proportions in her mind; now he was revealed as a violent and unscrupulous man, but not the murderer she had thought him to be.

'There are different ways of hurting children,' she said woodenly. 'Taking him from the only mother he remembers would hurt him.'

'I have to have the money,' he said desperately. 'Damn it, you don't understand! I need it! You owe it to me— I gave you house and home for fifteen years of your life!'

Drake broke in curtly, 'I rather think the contents of Olivia's trust fund were more than sufficient recompense for that act of generosity. However, if you give up all claim to Simon, I'll clean up your mess in Australia and see that you get an annuity.'

The older man's eyes flicked from Olivia's face to his. 'How much?' he asked.

Drake named a sum that brought a soft, hissing sigh to Olivia's lips.

Brian Harley laughed contemptuously. 'You must be joking.'

'That's all I'm prepared to offer,' Drake said, his voice crisp and emotionless.

'I think you must be forgetting that you have no claim to the boy. If I go ahead with this action—'

'Nobody is going to award custody to a cheat and a fraud, a man who is almost certainly going to end up in prison.'

'I need to think about it,' Brian Harley said, his eyes shifting. 'It's not a decision to—'

Olivia broke in, 'Drake, this is ridiculous! Why on earth should you pay out such an enormous sum of money—?'

'Darling,' he interrupted, smiling at her with warmth and charm, and a steely determination that only she could see, 'shut up and let me deal with this.'

Fuming, she obeyed.

Drake turned to the older man and said in a voice that pulled Olivia's skin tight, 'Make up your mind now. I'm going to withdraw my offer in two minutes.'

Half an hour later, after Brian Harley had reluctantly agreed, signed papers to relinquish all claim to custody and his trusteeship on grounds of ill-health, and taken himself and his solicitor off, Olivia looked up from the chair she had retired to and asked, 'Why are you prepared to pay out so much—and put yourself to such trouble—to get custody of Simon?'

His gaze pinned her to the chair. 'I thought you had that worked out. Revenge, of course. And the use of Simon's trust fund.'

She flinched, but ploughed on determinedly. 'I'm sorry I said that last night. I didn't mean it—not really. I was just so angry—' and hurt '—that I said the first thing that came to mind.' She flushed, but recovered, and finished, 'If you'd wanted revenge you wouldn't have offered to pull my stepfather out of the pit he's dug for himself.'

He opened the safe and pulled out the miniature, putting it down on the desk. The pretty, painted face looked out serenely, the eyes steady and very blue, a smile quirking the soft mouth.

Drake said levelly, 'I went to your flat that night to tell a greedy little fortune-hunter that there was no correspondence between my DNA and that of the child she was trying to pass off as mine. And then Simon walked into the room carrying this.'

Olivia pushed a hand through her hair. 'What did that have to do with anything?'

'My father bought this in some tiny country store the day he met my mother. He valued it very much—used to say that she had to be an ancestor because she had the same colour eyes as he did.'

'I don't understand,' she said blankly.

'Olivia, I am not my father's son—I'm adopted. My mother was unable to have children. She told me once that it almost broke their marriage up because she felt that she had let him down.'

She sank back into the chair, shaking her head. 'I didn't know that. But—what's it got to do with anything?'

'That's why there was no correspondence with the DNA. It had to have been my father who gave this miniature to your mother—he must have known she was pregnant and given her the one thing he had of value for her child.' He waited, then said deliberately, 'His child too.'

To Olivia's appalled horror, she put her head down in her hands and burst into tears, swamped by emotions so immense that she couldn't control them.

'Darling—don't,' he said, in a voice unlike any other she had ever heard from him.

She groped for her handkerchief, but even blowing her nose didn't seem to help.

'Bloody hell,' he said, and she felt herself being lifted in strong arms and carried across to the sofa. He sat down, lifted her into his lap, and held her closely so that she could weep her pain and frustration away in the comforting circle of his arms.

'But she told my stepfather it was you,' she wailed, when at last she had managed to get her sobs under control. 'Why did she do that?'

'Olivia, use your head. My father was in a hell of a situation. Mum was battling cancer, and her state of mind was vitally important. What do you think would have happened if she'd been told that not only had he slept with your mother, but that she was carrying a child—the child my mother had never been able to give him?

'I think my mother might have just given up. At the very least she would have been utterly disillusioned. I don't imagine either Elizabeth or Dad wanted that on their consciences. In fact, it could be why they didn't run away together. I was convenient—I'd already left the district so I couldn't be hurt. She couldn't have known that I was sending my money back from overseas for your stepfather to invest.'

Olivia blew her nose. 'It was a wicked thing to do.'

'She was desperate,' he said quietly. 'I suppose mine was the first name that came to mind. She was lovely, but she wasn't exactly sensible.'

'No,' Olivia said. Beautiful, and loving, and gracious, but not sensible. Elizabeth should have known her husband well enough to understand that his vindictiveness would ensure that Drake suffered for his supposed sin.

And within six months of Simon's birth Drake's father had died in a senseless accident, and Elizabeth had been left with a husband who bullied and abused her, and a daughter who, with the best will in the world, couldn't help her.

Drake said, 'At first I thought you were trying to foist your child onto me, but as soon as I saw the miniature I realised that Simon had to be my father's son. Your mother lied because she wanted to protect my father.'

'Do you think he—my stepfather knows this?'

'No,' he said.

'Why didn't you tell me?' she whispered. 'You kept so much secret. Why didn't you tell me that you weren't Simon's father?'

'There were several reasons,' he said grimly, 'but the most important was that I thought you might tell my mother.'

'I wouldn't have—' she said indignantly.

'I couldn't be sure of that, Don't forget that you'd threatened blackmail.'

It hurt, but viewed objectively he was right. 'I wouldn't have done it,' she said defensively. 'Anyway, you said your mother lives in Canada! How could I have told her?'

'I said she's *in* Canada. She's been on holiday there; she'll be back in three days. Her house is two streets away. I didn't know how she'd react to learning that my father not only had an affair the summer she was fighting for her life, but also had a child. I knew that if you carried out your threat and went to the newspapers, it would embarrass and upset her horribly. And, as it was obvious I owed some responsibility to Simon, I decided to let you go on thinking I was his father until I discovered what sort of person you were.'

She moved uneasily. Apparently he hadn't cared what her opinion of him had been.

'Stop that,' he said crisply. 'You didn't exactly seem like a grasping cheat, out for what you could get, and I had a faint suspicion that if you knew Simon wasn't mine you might take him away—especially after the grommets had gone in. And I definitely didn't want that by then.

'It was,' he added meditatively, 'a devil of a situation. I knew you despised me for the supposed affair, but I didn't really know whether it was because you thought I'd abandoned Elizabeth or whether, as I hoped, there was a more personal reason for it. If you remember, I did try to tell you before we got married, and got severely slapped down for my pains.'

'Oh,' she said, flushing. 'I thought you were going to tell me about your affair with my mother, and I couldn't *bear* it!'

He laughed softly. 'And I decided you simply weren't interested, that in spite of your encouraging response to my kisses the only thing that really meant anything to you was Simon's welfare.'

'Is that why you went all cold and nasty?'

'It didn't help that you were as arrogantly scathing as you could be. I thought, Damn her, she can be the one to come to me next time!'

It seemed to Olivia that the world stood poised and waiting on the edge of a precipice. Part of her told her that now was the time, but a hidden streak of cowardice whispered that if she failed she'd be left with nothing, not even hope. She hesitated, then asked slowly, 'Why did you want me to come to you?'

'Don't you know, Olivia?' His profile was etched against the bookshelves, a series of blunt lines and angles, powerful, masculine, dominating. 'I want you.'

The stark simplicity of his statement brought the blood to her face, but they weren't the words she wanted. 'Yet you've kept me at arm's length,' she retorted. 'Why?'

'Because instead of the experienced woman I assumed you were, you were very shy. You shied away from me like a nervous filly every time I came near you, and from your reactions I guessed that in spite of the two years you spent with a man you were a complete novice when it came to making love.' He looked across at her. 'Was the man you travelled with gay?'

'Yes. Neil's a darling, and I'm very fond of him. He kept me safe—taught me so much.'

'If he ever comes back from Australia I'd be glad to meet him.'

She looked at him suspiciously, but he seemed to mean it. 'Very macho men—'

'Don't generalise,' he returned evenly. 'I don't care to be called macho, nor homophobic. If you like him I imagine I will too.'

She nodded slowly. 'So you decided you didn't want a woman who wasn't up to scratch,' she said.

He smiled mockingly. 'So my conscience kicked in. I felt like a tired old satyr lying in wait to seduce a fresh, virginal young nymph.'

It was the last thing she had expected him to say. Her brows shot up and she laughed incredulously. 'I find that very hard to believe.'

'Then how about this?' he said, possessing himself of her slender hands. Almost musingly he said, 'I suppose I fell in love with you that summer when your mother and my father were indulging in their illicit affair, but it was obvious that it was my reputation that appealed to you. Dazzling the local tearaway is a far cry from marrying him. Anyway, you were just a baby so I put my hormones in cold storage and kept it light. You'll never know just how tempting you were, with your haughty little attempts at flirtation and your shocked response when I kissed you.

'When I left I decided that I'd come back one day and see how you were. But then my parents moved to Auckland, and the only time I went back to Springs Flat was when I fronted up to Harley. By then I was broke and cynical and murderously angry, and not looking for a wife or a lover. I never forgot you, but you were someone I'd left behind, not a real part of my life. And then, out of the blue, I got your spartan little letter.'

'Which made you very suspicious.'

'It had a distinct whiff of blackmail,' he agreed. 'So I came to see you. And I was appalled by the conditions you were living in, and furious with you for trying to blackmail me. But when it became obvious that either you were a bloody good actress or you really did think Simon was mine I decided to look further into the situation. So I told the private investigator to find out what had really happened seven years ago at Springs Flat.'

'But nobody else knew.'

He gave her an enigmatic glance. 'People always know more than you think. However, the Springs Flat trail had gone pretty cold, but he found out one strange thing. No one in Springs Flat knew you'd run away. Harley told them that you were shattered by your mother's death so he'd sent you to stay with friends in Auckland while he organised the sale of the house and the business. Then he simply packed up and went to Australia.'

'Very convenient,' she said, shivering.

'Very.' His voice was reflective. 'But my investigator also discovered that a year ago he hired a private detective to look for you and Simon, and that made me very curious. More intensive digging revealed the existence of the trust.'

'And you didn't know this until late last night?'

His smile was tigerish and hard. 'Not all of it, no.' With smooth grace he got to his feet pulling her upright with him, his arms linking loosely about her back. 'I had every intention of telling you that I was no relation of Simon that night at your flat. Then he appeared with the miniature and I realised what must have happened.'

He was looking down at her, half-closed eyes glinting with a passion she recognised, a hunger that sent little chills chasing each other up her spine.

Like a small, noisy dervish Simon came racing through the door. 'I'm going to be late for school!' he shouted. 'I have to go or my teacher will be mad.'

Drake laughed beneath his breath and released her. 'Goodbye, then—have a good day,' he said.

Simon hurtled across the room, kissed Olivia, then disappeared. Olivia listened to him calling Phillips down the hall. A fragile bubble of anticipation expanded within her breast. She didn't dare hope yet, but some tender emotion was stirring deep inside her.

'I'll go and make sure everything's all right,' Drake said.

A hand climbing to cover her heart with a fist, she watched him leave the room, tall and erect, broad shoulders carried high, with the lean, pantherish stride that did something odd to her bones.

Did he expect her to wait for him?

Probably. However, she couldn't simply hang around—she felt oddly shy, in need of a refuge.

So she walked sedately up to her bedroom. She had just finished making the bed when the door opened behind her. She didn't have to look to know who came in; those invisible antennae she seemed to have developed recently picked up Drake's aura.

She said, 'I truly didn't mean what I said last night. I was angry and hurt because you hadn't told me anything, and because I thought you'd put Simon in jeopardy.'

'I know. Olivia, look at me.'

It took a lot of willpower, but she turned and obeyed, her lips firmly held to hide their trembling, her eyes misty with hope.

'I love you,' he said steadily, his face completely without expression. 'Is there any hope that you might grow to love me one day?'

She lifted her eyes to his. 'I think I fell in love with you when I was fourteen,' she said simply. 'I've loved you ever since.'

She thought he might smile, that there might be joy in his face. She didn't expect him to close his eyes and open them to suspicious brightness, didn't expect to hear his voice roughen with shock and sensuality and laughter as he said, 'Thank God for that. I know I don't deserve it, but I'll never lie to you again, I swear.'

'Of course you won't,' she said, and went into his arms.

Some time later, she asked huskily, 'What about Phillips?'

'He's out for the day.' Their clothes had already been disposed of. He picked her up and put her onto the bed, coming down beside her.

'Don't you have to go to work?'

'Not today,' he said solemnly, and lowered his head to kiss the curve of her breast. His mouth lingered against the silken skin. 'You are so beautiful to me,' he said with quiet intensity. 'Warm and golden and sleek. When I first saw you again I thought about a description I'd read somewhere of an ancient ivory statue of Aphrodite—smooth-limbed and tawny-eyed with a smile that drove men to worship and madness.'

'You can't have,' she said, sliding her hands across the back of his head. 'I was haggard. I must have looked awful.'

'You were tired, but you were beautiful. And so valiant that you wrung my heart and made me furious at the same time. You will always be beautiful, because your loveliness comes from inside you.'

His hand moved down, caressed her hip, slid between her legs. Already exquisitely excited, Olivia shivered at his gentle touch. 'Trust me,' he whispered.

'I'll always trust you,' she said. 'I trusted you enough to ask you to marry me. I'll trust you all my life, with everything I have, everything I am...'

Sensation spiralled through her. She gasped, and he said in a shaken voice, 'My heart, my dearest love, my golden girl, I can't—'

She looked up into his face—the burnished olive skin, the saturnine brows, the heavy-lidded eyes, pure green now, and filled with a leaping turbulence, a heated need that evoked a similar hunger from her.

Smiling, she pulled him into her, her hands across the wide expanse of his shoulders, her hips moving to meet that first slow, controlled thrust. It didn't hurt, or only for a moment, and then he had passed the frail barrier and she was being taken over by his male strength and gentleness, lost in the magic wrought by her body responding to the sheer physical mastery of his, lost in her heart's freedom to love and be loved.

It couldn't last, she thought feverishly, astounded at her body's capacity to feel; such ecstasy must have a culmination soon. But Drake set the pace, using superb restraint until at last the forces that racked her so magnificently imploded in a firestorm that had her call out incoherently and arch upwards. Almost immediately he followed her, and locked together, joined in body as in soul, they came quietly down from those rarefied heights.

'What were you dreaming about?' he asked later, gathering her close as she woke from a short sleep.

She lay silent, basking in the heat of his body, in the lingering remnants of the languorous satisfaction that still melted her bones. 'It wasn't a nightmare,' she said huskily. 'It was very vivid, though. I dreamed of the woman in the miniature.'

He kissed her forehead. 'And what was she doing?' he asked, humouring her.

'She was reciting poetry.'

His chest lifted in laughter. 'What? "Young Lochinvar"? No, that would be after her time. Something from "The Rape of the Lock"?'

Smiling, she ran the tip of her tongue across a hard swell of muscle in his shoulder. 'No. As near as I can remember, it went like this:

> *I found my Love as you have yours,*
> *And know it will be true,*
> *My Portrait is the fated charm*

That sped your Love to you.

But if you be not Fortune's Fool
Now your Heart's Desire is nigh,
Pass on my likeness as Cupid's Tool
Or your Love will fade and die.'

'She was,' he said drily, 'no poet.'

'No, which makes it seem almost authentic. It's the sort of thing that a young woman of fashion—which she so obviously was—might try her hand at writing. I wonder who she was.'

'An unknown woman,' Drake said, even more drily.

'I wonder if she told your father the same thing she told me,' Olivia said. 'To pass on the miniature when he'd found his love . . .'

His brows rose. 'I wouldn't have put you down as superstitious, darling.'

'I don't think I am,' she said doubtfully. 'At least, if I am, it's only about her. She told me to write to you, you know.'

He rolled over onto his back, taking her with him so that she lay on top of him, her bones lax, her whole being humming with a deep, inner contentment. 'In a dream?'

She knew that he was laughing at her, but continued thoughtfully, 'Yes. And if Simon hadn't come out with her that night in the flat you'd have told me that the DNA test proved that he and you had no blood relationship at all and you'd have left, wouldn't you?'

'I doubt it.' He grinned at her astonished face. 'I wanted you right from the start. I think this was inevitable, although I'll confess I wasn't ready to accept that I loved you. We probably would have wasted a lot of time, and I'll admit that the miniature helped there. As soon as I saw it I knew the only person who could have given it to your mother was my father.'

Coincidence? Of course it was—just one of those odd little quirks in time. Looked at with the cool eye of logic, there was absolutely no way the woman in the miniature could have been manipulating circumstances. She was from another time, half a world away. To accept such a ludicrous idea one would have to believe in the occult— and there was certainly no stench of brimstone about the miniature.

And yet...

'I think we should give it away.'

'Olivia—'

Olivia kissed the arrogant line of his jaw. 'Your father kept it,' she said, 'and things didn't go right for him and your mother.'

His hands came up to frame her face, his thumbs pushing up her chin so that he could see her expression. 'Do you honestly believe that our happiness depends on getting rid of a miniature portrait?'

She reacted to the steel in his voice with perfect honesty, meeting his eyes, trying to show him that she was serious. 'No.' Only one word, but she didn't need to expand; her voice rang with conviction. 'However, I think we should give her the chance to do what she does so well—make antagonists into lovers.'

'Kiss me again.'

She did so, forgetting about the portrait, giving her whole self into the kiss. Once more the shimmering tide of passion began to rise, aching through her legs, pooling into a heated coil at the base of her stomach, filling her veins with honey and her heart with a slow, primal need.

'All right,' he said when she broke the kiss. 'You can get rid of it.'

'Just like that?' She wriggled experimentally on him. 'Do you mean that all I have to do to get my own way is kiss you?'

His laughter was soft and untrammelled, free of suspicion or mistrust, incredibly sexy. His long fingers tightened on her hips, holding her in place so that she could feel the rapid burgeoning of his need. 'Yes,' he said deeply. 'I'm putty in your hands. Didn't you know?'

'That doesn't feel like putty. Of course, it isn't in my hands. Shall I...?'

A strenuous and eventful half-hour or so afterwards, she sighed and snuggled close. 'It feels more like putty now,' she said thoughtfully.

'Give me a few minutes...'

Laughing, she rubbed her cheek against the delicious friction of his chest hair. 'I can't believe that I'm lying here making innuendoes; it just isn't my style. It's very disconcerting.' Then, in a quick change of mood, she murmured, 'How lucky we are, you and I. I don't suppose anyone has ever been so happy as we are, do you?'

'I certainly haven't.' His arms tightened around her. 'And I fully intend to go on being just as happy as this for the rest of our lives. How are you going to get rid of the mysterious miniature?'

'Perhaps we should just leave her lying about somewhere.'

'You realise how valuable she is?'

'I don't think we should sell her,' she said firmly. 'But we could make it easy for her to go. I think she'll probably let us know.'

'Hmm,' he said thoughtfully. 'All right. Now, forget about the wretched thing and tell me again how much you love me.'

It was something she never tired of saying, because he was endlessly inventive, repaying her open love and desire with his own heated words and thoughtful actions. Already she was planning the hundreds, thousands of ways she could tell him and show him in the years that unrolled before them, fair and full of promise. Love had transformed their mirror marriage—picture-perfect and shallow and two-dimensional—into a real one.

Yet even as she bent her will to the task she offered a small thanksgiving to the unknown woman who had found her love and somehow down the centuries, confounding logic and reality, seemed to be making it possible for others to find theirs.

* * * * *

Look out next month for Anet Carruthers'
encounter with THE MARRIAGE MAKER in
Meant to Marry

MILLS & BOON

AUGUST 1996 HARDBACK TITLES

Romance

Reckless Flirtation *Helen Brooks*	H4500	0 263 14866 1
Family Man *Rosemary Carter*	H4501	0 263 14927 7
Married to the Man *Ann Charlton*	H4502	0 263 14868 8
Runaway Wedding *Ruth Jean Dale*	H4503	0 263 14928 5
The Mirror Bride *Robyn Donald*	H4504	0 263 14807 6
Best Man to Wed? *Penny Jordan*	H4505	0 263 14873 4
Clanton's Woman *Patricia Knoll*	H4506	0 263 14930 7
The Best Man for Linzi *Miriam MacGregor*	H4507	0 263 14846 7
The Marriage Risk *Debbie Macomber*	H4508	0 263 14875 0
The Only Man for Maggie *Leigh Michaels*	H4509	0 263 14931 5
Carmichael's Return *Lilian Peake*	H4510	0 263 14877 7
With his Ring *Jessica Steele*	H4511	0 263 14879 3
His Cousin's Wife *Lynsey Stevens*	H4512	0 263 14850 5
Avoiding Mr Right *Sophie Weston*	H4513	0 263 14880 7
Wedding Fever *Lee Wilkinson*	H4514	0 263 14925 0
A Suitable Mistress *Cathy Williams*	H4515	0 263 14881 5

Historical Romance

Betrayed Hearts *Elizabeth Henshall*	M389	0 263 15011 9
The Wolf's Promise *Alice Thornton*	M390	0 263 15012 7

MEDICAL ROMANCE

LOVE ON CALL

The Real Fantasy *Caroline Anderson*	D307	0 263 14995 1
Taking It All *Sharon Kendrick*	D308	0 263 14996 X

MILLS & BOON

AUGUST 1996 LARGE PRINT TITLES

Romance

Prisoner of Passion *Lynne Graham*	927	0 263 14664 2
Desperately Seeking Annie *Patricia Knoll*	928	0 263 14665 0
Hot Blood *Charlotte Lamb*	929	0 263 14666 9
A Woman to Remember *Miranda Lee*	930	0 263 14667 7
Spring Bride *Sandra Marton*	931	0 263 14668 5
Taming a Tycoon *Leigh Michaels*	932	0 263 14669 3
The Bachelor Chase *Emma Richmond*	933	0 263 14670 7
A Wife in Waiting *Jessica Steele*	934	0 263 14671 5

Historical Romance

Daring Deception *Brenda Hiatt*	0 263 14760 6
The Outrageous Dowager *Sarah Westleigh*	0 263 14761 4

MEDICAL ROMANCE

LOVE ON CALL

A Fresh Diagnosis *Jessica Matthews*	0 263 14692 8
Bound by Honour *Josie Metcalfe*	0 263 14693 6
Unexpected Complications *Joanna Neil*	0 263 14694 4
Cruise Doctor *Stella Whitelaw*	0 263 14695 2

TEMPTATION

Forms of Love *Rita Clay Estrada*	0 263 14960 9
Happy Birthday, Baby *Leandra Logan*	0 263 14961 7

MILLS & BOON®

SEPTEMBER 1996 HARDBACK TITLES

Romance

The Trophy Wife *Rosalie Ash*	H4516	0 263 14938 2
Honeymoon Assignment *Sally Carr*	H4517	0 263 14939 0
Meant to Marry *Robyn Donald*	H4518	0 263 14941 2
No More Secrets *Catherine George*	H4519	0 263 14942 0
Rebel in Disguise *Lucy Gordon*	H4520	0 263 14943 9
Where There's a Will *Day Leclaire*	H4521	0 263 14944 7
Aunt Lucy's Lover *Miranda Lee*	H4522	0 263 14946 3
Daddy's Little Helper *Debbie Macomber*	H4523	0 263 14947 1
Living With the Enemy *Laura Martin*	H4524	0 263 14948 X
One-Man Woman *Carole Mortimer*	H4525	0 263 14949 8
His Sleeping Partner *Elizabeth Oldfield*	H4526	0 263 14951 X
Jilted Bride *Elizabeth Power*	H4527	0 263 14952 8
First-Time Father *Emma Richmond*	H4528	0 263 14953 6
Desert Wedding *Alexandra Scott*	H4529	0 263 14954 4
Dominic's Child *Catherine Spencer*	H4530	0 263 14964 1
Once Burned *Margaret Way*	H4531	0 263 14965 X

Historical Romance™

The Rainborough Inheritance *Helen Dickson*	M391	0 263 15015 1
The Last Gamble *Mary Nichols*	M392	0 263 15016 X

Medical Romance™

The Ideal Choice *Caroline Anderson*	D309	0 263 15001 1
More than Skin-Deep *Margaret O'Neill*	D310	0 263 15002 X

MILLS & BOON®

SEPTEMBER 1996 LARGE PRINT TITLES

Romance

Last Stop Marriage *Emma Darcy*	935	0 263 14712 6
Husband Material *Emma Goldrick*	936	0 263 14713 4
The Colorado Countess *Stephanie Howard*	937	0 263 14714 2
A Simple Texas Wedding *Ruth Jean Dale*	938	0 263 14715 0
Untamed Lover *Sharon Kendrick*	939	0 263 14716 9
Relative Sins *Anne Mather*	940	0 263 14717 7
A Faulkner Possession *Margaret Way*	941	0 263 14718 5
A Night to Remember *Anne Weale*	942	0 263 14719 3

Historical Romance™

Farewell the Heart *Meg Alexander*	0 263 14776 2
A Biddable Girl? *Paula Marshall*	0 263 14777 0

And Daughter Makes Three *Caroline Anderson*	0 263 14726 6
A Question of Trust *Maggie Kingsley*	0 263 14727 4
The Disturbing Dr Sheldon *Elisabeth Scott*	0 263 14728 2
Consultant Care *Sharon Wirdnam*	0 263 14729 0

TEMPTATION™

A Kiss in the Dark *Tiffany White*	0 263 14962 5
Undercover Baby *Gina Wilkins*	0 263 14963 3

White River Regional Library
368 E. Main Stre
Batesville, A

DISCARD

Independence County Library
368 E. Main Street
Batesville, AR 72501